A H
DOOMED
BY FATE

BY

MAZE

A HEART DOOMED BY FATE

A HEART DOOMED BY FATE

1st edition published:

April 27, 2024

Editing by:

Esther E. Schmidt & Virginia Tesi Carey

Beta readers:

Lynne & Wendy

Formatting & Designer:

Esther E. Schmidt

For readers who have a ghost hunting heart,
and who crave the creepiest adventures.

CHAPTER 01

ARTSY

"I really need to go now. I can't be late for school." I smile as I look at my reflection in the mirror in front of me.

"Good luck, honey," my mother replies in a sweet tone.

My mom passed away when I was thirteen. Yes, I know it sounds insane because I'm staring at her reflection in the mirror, but let me explain something that happened exactly five years ago today. My throat burns and my eyes turn watery when I think about it. Losing her still hurts even though five years have passed.

Before she died, she looked me in the eye, held my hand tightly in hers, and told me, *"There is one thing I need to tell you. On your birthday last year, do you remember the black rose I showed you? The one with the red lines crossing the petals? It isn't just a simple rose that I wanted you to place in your grandparents' attic to cheer the place up."* She coughed, the sound rough and hard, indicating her body had difficulties holding on to life.

I was so confused by her words, I didn't understand what she meant by it. Getting the rose was a pretty gift. I still remember when I caught its scent the first time. Even now it looks pretty as it sits in front of the window. But to have another real and powerful meaning? It's the last thing you would think of when you're getting a simple rose.

She continued to tell me, *"Artsy. Please, promise me you will take good care of it, and look after yourself. It's really important. You can stay at your grandparents, they will take care of you. I love you."* Those were the last words she gave me right before her final breath left her body.

Her eyes became empty right after that sentence while I bawled out mine. I crumbled to the floor and couldn't believe I lost her. After I cried beside her for several minutes, I pulled myself together and wiped away my tears in anger.

I sprinted through the rain toward my grandparents' house. Just like my mom told me to do. My grandma took me in with open arms because I couldn't live on my own at the mere age of thirteen. My parents were both dead, and now I had no one except for my grandparents.

I kept the rose as a reminder of my mom. I never moved it from its place on the wooden table in front of the window in the attic.

And here I am, exactly five years later, staring at my own reflection in the mirror with my mom standing behind me with a bright smile on her face. She's clearly proud of how far I've come by myself.

It was pretty hysterical when I saw her for the first time popping up behind me as a reflection in the mirror. Though, once she explained it to me, it all made sense. Well, it had to sink in after her death because it was pretty hard to believe.

The rose she gave me on my birthday is special and connects us. Though, it's linked to my heart, and that's the tricky part I have to be really careful with.

If someone would touch the rose, harm it in any way, or so much as destroy it? I will feel every bit of it and ultimately my heart will stop. It's interesting, unbelievable, crazy to say the least, but also very scary.

The one thing I'm thankful for is the fact that I still have contact with my mom in some way. At least, when I stare at my reflection I can. It's like an emotional bond we share. The rose is the connection, and it gives me the ability to talk to her.

"See you later." I shoot her a grin and get to my feet.

I wipe the dust off my knee-high socks that comes from the cracks in the wooden floor in the attic. My eyes find the mirror to glance at my mother one more time, but she's already gone.

"Time is up." I sigh.

After five years it's still hard to accept she's not really with me anymore. I snatch my backpack from the floor and throw it over my shoulder as I stalk toward the door. I pass the table with my rose sitting on top of it, surrounded by the glass dome I placed over it for protection.

I bounce down the stairs and yell, "I'm going," from the hallway at my grandma who is sitting in the living room watching TV with the volume on loud.

I open the door and let the freezing air welcome me. It's ridiculous that I need to wear this skirt with a cropped blouse as my school uniform. The only good thing is that we have knee-high socks and a blazer but it's still way too cold for this weather. The boys have suits, and to be honest? I'd rather be wearing that right now too.

I shiver as I step outside and start to walk to school. Thankfully, it's not that far from my house. I'm glad I don't have to take the bus or even my bicycle, it's just a few blocks and I'm already standing in front of the building.

"Hey," I bellow when I see a hint of a blonde girl.

She's dressed in the same uniform as me, but she has her hair up in a bun. She turns to see who shouted and our eyes meet. I quickly shove my hand in the air to give her a wave. A hint of a smile slides across her face as soon as she sees me, but it quickly disappears when her cheeks turn red from embarrassment. She dismisses me and gives her attention back to the boy she was talking to.

Jane. She was my best friend since I was born. My mom and hers were best friends as well when they met in high school. Because they were so close, Jane and I grew up with each other. Ever since my mom passed away, Jane doesn't seem to care about me at all. She can't even stand to look at me for more than a second. It's as if she never liked me and only faked our friendship for as long as my mother was alive.

I'm used to it by now. Everyone in this school thinks I'm a freak for what happened to my mom, and how I am dealing with it. They know nothing about anything, and still they judge me.

I drop my head with a sigh and glance at my black leather boots. I stomp into school and hear a flow of laughter and gasps around me. I keep telling myself it's okay because this happens every day.

I should be able to deal with it by now with all these kids laughing right in my face and talking about me as soon as I turn my back on them. All of it leaves me with a hollow feeling inside my chest. It hurts to know there's no one out there who actually cares how I'm doing.

All I can hope when I stroll through the hallway, surrounded by people who hate me, is that the bell rings soon, telling me it's time to go home. My safe haven. The place where I can sit in the attic and look in the mirror to see my one and only friend; my mom.

I let my bag drop from my shoulder and fish out three books I need for class as I keep walking in the direction of the classroom.

I hold the books tightly in my hands and don't really pay attention to the kids around me. I like being in my own world–my own thoughts. It's way better than focusing on the mess surrounding me.

The only downside is the random bump against the shoulder from others not watching where they are going. Only this time I feel someone hitting my books with force causing for them to fall out of my hands and land with a loud smack on the floor. My eyes fly up to see who did it.

"Hudson," I whisper to myself, seeing the popular school bully standing in front of me.

His blond hair is pulled back way too slick with probably an entire jar of gel. He has blue cyan eyes, and that stupid, everlasting smirk on his face. He's too handsome, and I guess it makes up for the jerkiness he had inside of him.

"What?" he spits, with his amazing British accent that I really shouldn't like, but it does something to me whenever I hear him talk.

I've known Hudson for a little over a year now. Every girl is standing in line for him. He's the popular guy, but he's far from perfect. I wish I could hate him, I really do, but there's something about him that causes butterflies to flutter inside my belly.

I swallow hard, embarrassed of the fact that he heard me whisper his name. I have no idea what to say to him. My lips are glued together due to the tiny crush I have on him.

"That's what I thought." He snickers, and his friends behind him give him a big smirk.

I feel miserable, how can people act like this? More importantly, why do I let him bully me? All I want is to be left alone. I hate it here. I want to go home.

"See you in class, loser." Hudson shoots me a wink.

It's not a cute, flirty wink. Nope. It's a wink that tells me he isn't done bullying me yet. I reach for my books and squat down to the floor. I don't even have the energy anymore to move or get up to pull myself to class. These little altercations ruin my entire day, my entire week, my entire freaking life.

"Hurry up, you're in my way," he snaps with irritation.

I flinch, I can't help it. I hate people who yell at me. It's horrible. He is so tall, so powerful, looming over me as if I'm a fly he's about to squash.

"Sorry," I hiss through my teeth and place my hand on one of the books to slide it toward me.

"Good girl." He grins and strolls past me.

Hudson glances over his shoulder to check on his buddies who are still standing around me.

"Come on guys, let her be." He waves at his friends, indicating for them to follow him.

"Wait for it," one of them growls.

I ignore him, and keep my eyes focused on the floor in front of me. I don't want to look at either one and I wish they'd just go away already. They finally do, but not before lashing out one more time.

The same guy who growled at me decides to use my finger as part of the floor as he walks past me. His full weight causes a sharp pain to shoot through my finger, up my arm, and causes a hot flash throughout my body. I bite my lip, trying not to scream, cry, or yell at him. Knowing it would only make things worse.

"Dude," Hudson snaps at his friend, noticing what he did.

"What? She deserves it," he replies, and snickers as he walks past Hudson.

"Come on man, she's nothing," the other guy tells Hudson and quickly dashes after the other guy.

I ignore all of them and hold my finger close to my chest as I stare at my books that are still scattered across the floor. I should have listened when my grandma said this school wasn't for me, but it was this or homeschool. I don't want to be homeschooled. I would live a lonely life with no friends at all. Not that this is any better, but at least I'm trying not to be a complete hermit.

I hear Hudson mutter something behind me. Why hasn't he left yet? The others are always around him, and he's rarely alone. The others already stepped inside the classroom, so what is he still doing here?

The bell rings, shit. Class is starting, I need to go in before I am too late. I am never late, because then I'll be in the spotlight. I hate it when people look at me, it makes me anxious, especially when I enter a classroom full of people. I can't handle that. I need to leave.

I quickly snatch the books off the floor and shove them into my bag before I stand from the dirty floor. I swipe the tears from my eyes, anger bubbling up inside me as I spin on my heels. Expecting to face an empty hallway, I'm caught by surprise when I bump into someone.

"My bad, sorry," I croak, and keep my head down, still overemotional about what just happened.

The person in front of me stays quiet. I clear my throat, embarrassed by the new situation I'm caught in as I glance up to meet the same cyan eyes again. Shit, it's Hudson.

"Hey," he murmurs.

14

A HEART DOOMED BY FATE

His appearance isn't as standoffish as he normally is. He seems more calm, at ease. His eyes hold warmth, as if he doesn't hate me. Weird. Is he here to offer an apology? Did he regret his bully moment or did he stick around to rub it in some more?

"Hi." I sniff, uncomfortable with having him close.

Who knows what he's up to. There's no way I trust a guy who was an ass to me two freaking seconds ago.

"I just—" he starts, but shuts his mouth just as fast.

What is going on? It's strange to be alone and this close to Hudson. And why does it suddenly feel as if he's trying to be nice to me?

"What's wrong?" I ask, trying to keep my voice neutral.

I've never had a normal conversation with Hudson. There must be something going on, why else would he suddenly be talking to me when he normally won't give me the time of day. Unless of course he and his friends need a laugh and bully me for their own personal entertainment.

"I'm not going to apologize," he snaps, eyes piercing me with a hard look before he adds, "But, what Roan did wasn't okay, and I want you to know that I don't stand behind his actions."

His voice is tight and his face shows regret. The way his hands clench and unclench, the muscle in his jaw jumps…it's clear he isn't used to admitting the things he just threw at me.

"Thanks?" I say in confusion.

I fidget with my fingers, anxiety getting the better of me with him still standing close and the weird situation we're both caught in.

"I need to go to class, are you coming or what?" he questions, pointing at the door of the classroom.

"No, thanks." I offer him a hint of a warm smile.

He raises his eyebrow and asks, "Why not? Are you going to skip class when you're already here?"

I'm sure he's just making conversation, or maybe he is curious. Either way, I can't give him the true reason I'm skipping class. After all, he's the school bully. That is his reputation. Telling someone like him your secrets, your issues, your problems? It's a sure way for things not to end well.

I'm pretty sure the whole school will know the second the words spill over my lips, and my life is hell as it is. So, no thank you; my lips are staying sealed.

"C'mon, what's the reason?" He gives me a flirty smile while he lets his gaze slide over my body from my toes to the crown of my head.

My breathing picks up the way his eyes linger on my lips.

Feeling uncomfortable and getting annoyed by the whole situation, I snap a little too harsh, "It's none of your business."

He narrows his eyes. "Whatever. I didn't care anyway."

His face closes off and turns back to the old, harsh Hudson he always is.

I sigh, this guy. If the sky holds all the sweetness, and the ground is filled with rudeness...then Hudson is definitely lying flat on his back, becoming one with the damn ground.

I stare as I watch him walk away. There's determination in his movement, confidence in each step as his hair bounces around, not caring at all, just like the man it's attached to. His strong, spicy cologne still lingers around me. I should hate him, I really should. And maybe I do deep down. But I also can't stop admiring him. He's perfect in his own way.

A HEART DOOMED BY FATE

HUDSON

Class was boring. I received a warning for being late, but I don't really care. Hell, if it was anyone else, they would receive detention or other disciplinary actions. It's a part of being popular I think, because somehow I've never received detention like the other guys I hang out with.

"What took you so long, dude?" Roan asks me when we walk out of school together.

I bet he has been waiting to ask me that question for over an hour. I'm glad our seats are far away from each other in class.

"I had to deal with something," I reply, and glance to the left to locate my bike.

And there she is…and there she is as well. My bike, and Artsy who is sitting by herself against the tree, staring at the flowers that surround her in the grass. She always simply sits there after school. I have no clue what's so entertaining about watching flowers, but I guess it's her thing.

"Remember, rehearsal around seven." Roan grins as we bump our fists and head for our bikes.

I throw my leg over my bike and fire it up. Rehearsal today is very important. We have to rehearse the set for Wednesday. Me and the band have a concert, but the only problem is…we need one more song to finish our new album. And we only have two days left to finish it.

I blink a few times and realize I've been staring at the girl sitting by the tree for minutes while I was stuck inside my head. Shit, what if she saw me watching her? Imagine how awkward it would be to explain my gawking. Worse, what if other people saw me looking at her? Oh, shit. I need to get out of here.

I quickly ride off and head in the direction of our studio. Maybe it's better to arrive a bit early. At least it will give me some extra time to work on a new song. I am the lead singer, the songwriter, and play lead guitar. Roan plays drums, and does some background music together with Steve, who plays bass.

I arrive at the studio, still no idea what I could write a song about. I had two weeks to write one, and now I only have two days. I'm such an idiot for putting it off while I should have been working on one.

I park my bike and unlock the door to get inside of the building. Sitting on the couch with some water from the fridge I take out my phone and pull up the notes app.

"C'mon, Hudson, think," I mutter to myself.

All my mind can think about is what happened at school with Artsy. How we bullied her, how she ran off, and how I saw her sitting by herself surrounded by flowers like she does every day. Shit never gets physical, not the way things escalated today. A few words here and there, teasing for fun. Harmless.

Everyday stuff, just like the way she heads for the field of flowers to sit by herself, ignoring everything and everyone around her. Maybe it's her way to find some peace and quiet. Who knows? It might even be a girl thing, and I'll never understand.

"Hey, man," Roan quips as he and Steve enter the room with the loud noise of the front door slamming close behind them.

"Sup." I stand and close the app that's still lacking the words to throw a song together.

"And? Did you come up with something?" Steve asks before he so much as takes a seat.

"Nope. What about you guys? Any inspiration I can work with?" I ask, handing out bottles of water.

"Nah." Roan shakes his head.

"We'll come up with something. At least, you always do. And if you don't? Then that's fine too, right? It'll just be one song less than the other albums. Whatever." Steve shrugs and takes a sip from his water.

"What he said," Roan agrees.

"I'll think about it." I sigh.

I'm the leader of this band, so I have the final say in what happens.

"Let's just rehearse our setlist for now until someone comes up with a new idea," I suggest, grabbing my guitar.

"Sure," they agree in sync.

Roan slides behind the drums and Steve gets his hands on the other microphone while slinging the strap over his head and adjusting his bass guitar. Hours pass. We rehearse all the songs until night has fallen. But it's worth it; we're absolutely ready for our concert on Wednesday. Except, no one came up with a new idea for a song.

"Goodnight guys, see you tomorrow," we say to each other, exchanging some fist bumps before we leave the building to head for our motorcycles.

I am the last one to leave and as I ride back home it's raining hard and it takes me awhile to get back home.

"I'm home," I yell after I've parked my motorcycle inside the garage and slip into the house.

Water is dripping down from my hair and clothes, leaving a puddle where I stand as I take off my jacket.

"How was school, honey?" my mom asks and hands me a towel as she strides into the kitchen.

"It was okay, nothing much happened," I reply, taking the towel to dry off my dripping hair.

"Are you hungry?" she asks.

"Nah, thanks. I think I'm just going to crash." I give her a soft smile and hand the towel back to her.

"Okay. Goodnight, baby." She smiles and gives me a soft kiss on the crown of my head.

I jog up the stairs. I'm so tired from this day, rehearsal was tough. It always is a few days before a concert. We need to start planning instead of just winging it at the last second. It takes so much energy.

I take off my wet clothes, changing into a pair of sweatpants as I drop myself onto the bed. It doesn't take much time before my eyes fall shut and my body drags me into a deep sleep.

The loud blaring of my alarm bounces off the wall in the early morning.

"Stop it," I groan and groggily rollover in an effort to smack the damn alarm clock off the nightstand.

"Ugh," I grumble as I miss and force myself to throw my legs off the mattress, smacking the alarm clock with my flat hand to turn it off.

Today is the final day to create a song to add to the album. The pressure and small timeframe is going to be hard. It's a day filled with work and nothing else. First, though? School.

I dash to my closet and quickly snatch a clean school uniform to wear today. I throw a hoodie over it with a logo from my band on it. The alarm I set gave me maximum sleep time and only a small timeframe to get dressed, which now makes me late.

I scoop my bag with books off the ground and head down the stairs. I usually skip breakfast and just buy something at school, or at the store along the way if I have some spare time left. So, just like any other day, I get on my bike and leave the house without so much as a goodbye; my parents are used to it by now.

When I park my bike at school I find the entire schoolyard void of people. Not a single person is hanging around. What the heck is going on? Either I'm too late, too early, or something else is going on.

I swing my leg off my bike when someone runs in my direction. He grabs my arm and gives it a tiny pull to get my attention. I turn my head at the guy and groan, ready to snap at the idiot.

"You need to come inside," the young guy yells.

He's clutching his phone and the screen tells me he was taking a video of something.

"What's going on?" I question and raise my eyebrow.

"Just look for yourself, follow me," he rambles and gives my arm another tug to get me to move.

I rush after him and finally see where all the people are. The entire hallway is crowded by folks clutching their phone, not a single teacher in sight.

In the middle of the gathering are two people I instantly recognize. My pals, Roan and Steve. But there is someone else. It looks like a girl. She is sitting on the ground in her oversized hoodie over her school uniform. Her hands are covering her face while her legs are shaking underneath her body.

I reach for the person nearby to grab his arm and demand, "What is this?"

"It's Roan and Steve," he rattles with a huge smile waving his phone at me to show how eager he's videoing and enjoying the show.

"Yeah, no shit. But what are they doing?" I snap.

Aggravated by the situation, I grab him by the collar which almost causes him to drop his phone.

"Okay, okay. Calm down, dude. The girl bumped into Roan and it made his phone fall from his hand. The screen is completely shattered. He got pissed and called Steve, and then this happened. I have no idea what they are going to do but it's entertaining," the guy eagerly explains, trying to get my hand off him so he can focus back on documenting the whole thing.

"What?" I snarl.

And this is why I can never leave these two idiots alone. They always cause trouble. I mean, I get Roan is angry, phones are expensive. But c'mon, bumping into someone? Nine out of ten times it's an accident. I have no reason to believe she meant to break his phone.

I always had my eye on her, and she simply isn't the kind of person to be vindictive. Hell, she avoids people at every turn.

Yeah, Roan and Steve are my friends. I've known them for years, we have a band together, and we spend most of our free time together. But I can't let this happen. This girl looks terrified. I bet she can't even show her face at school again after this incident. I can't let them do this to her. If I thought yesterday went too far? This situation surely beats it.

So, I decide to follow my gut and step through the crowd to get to my two friends. They are laughing at her, throwing food in her face as they bark mean things to degrade her some more.

"Enough," I growl, and push them aside to get them away from the girl.

I hear all the people gasp from my action. My heart races inside my chest as I try to think of the right way to contain the situation.

"What the hell, dude," Roan bellows with a load of fire in his voice.

I bet they didn't expect their best friend to stop them. I glance over to check on the girl. Her head tilts slightly back to see what's going on around her until her puffy, red eyes meet mine. She looks completely destroyed. Cheeks wet from crying, her hair in a mess and sticking to her face, and her clothes are dirty.

I swallow hard at the lump in my throat. A turmoil of feelings hit me to see her this way and I'm not liking it at all. I feel bad for her. Before this moment I never thought about what it's like to be in her shoes and endure the teasing and games we do whenever we run into her.

Sure, it never got physical until yesterday and today, but it's hurting her either way. The damage is done, and I feel terrible for her.

I turn my head toward my friend who is puffing out his breaths to indicate how angry he still is.

"Just let her be. She's not worth your time," I tell him to avoid a head-on confrontation because that sure won't solve anything.

"You're right. I'm not wasting my breath on you one damn second longer," he angrily spits at Artsy who is now crawled up against my locker.

Her head lifts up fully this time. She gives me one last look before she jumps to her feet and runs off, bumping into everyone who's blocking her path. Shit.

"Artsy," I yell after her as I watch her disappear into the crowd.

"I'll be right back," I grunt in the direction of Roan and Steve.

I jump into a run and follow into the direction I watched Artsy disappear in. I have to find her. I have no idea where she might have gone. I don't even know her, let alone know where she might have disappeared to when something bad happened.

I come to a stop and suddenly realize I do know where she might be. Every day when I get on my bike I notice her sitting by the tree in the middle of a field filled with flowers. It would make sense to look for her there. I quickly rush to the place where I parked my bike earlier.

"Artsy?" I bellow and glance around.

Relief fills me when I spot her near the tree. I stalk toward her. She's sitting in the high grass, not caring at all about the stains it will leave on her clothes. On the other hand, her hoodie is already stained from the food the guys threw at her.

Her head whips up when I'm close and it shows her pale face. Guilt hits me hard and causes shock waves to flow through my veins. I hate seeing her like this and my stomach knots at the reminder of what this girl has to endure. Not only what my friends did yesterday and today... but what I've done as well.

I never realized.

Never intended.

How the hell did it get so far as to hurt and break her like the emotionally shattered girl in front of me?

ARTSY

My vision is blurry due to my tears, but I catch a glimpse of Hudson's blond hair and furiously blink and wipe my eyes when I mutter, "Hudson?"

My voice is hoarse from crying. What is he doing here? I thought for sure he was going to stay with his friends. I mean, it was kind enough for him to break up their torment so I was able to escape. Though, he has always been the one who also actively participated. Not the physical part, but verbally for sure.

"Artsy," he says, completely out of breath as if he's been running to catch up with me.

Remembering our last altercation after his buddy stepped on my fingers, I hiss, "You're not going to say sorry, so what are you doing here?"

I don't care if I hurt his feelings. At this point, I hate his friends and by default hate him as well. Maybe he didn't do anything, but I heard his words loud and clear when he said I wasn't worth talking to. I think those very words cut deep and hurt me more than his friends making fun of me in front of the whole school.

Ugh, who am I kidding? The stupid crush I have on him will forgive the idiot within seconds. It doesn't matter what he does to me, my feelings for him won't go away. Every time I hope his actions will cross a line that will make me hate him. I should. Maybe…maybe I do because it can't go on like this.

"I'm, I'm sorry," he stutters and lets himself drop to his knees onto the grass right beside me.

This is definitely new. I've never heard him say sorry before; not to me or to anyone else. I figure he considers it a sign of weakness, and Hudson isn't weak. At least, that's the impression he gives everyone around him.

My eyes widen as if my brain is still trying to catch up and I mutter, "What?" I blink at him and quickly add, "It wasn't your fault."

He keeps silent for a couple of breaths before he says, "But still. I feel guilty for how I treated you the past few months."

His raspy voice mixed with his accent fills my ears. My stomach flips and I feel warmth spread inside my chest. Shit. Why does this guy get to me? He's a bully, just like his shitty friends and yet here my heart goes with skipping a beat when he gives me a handful of sweet words that form an apology for the things he did.

I must be crazy, but I also can't stop the small smile from sliding across my face when I softly tell him, "Thanks."

Sadness hits me when I realize how pathetic this situation really is. How pathetic I am for feeling happy within this moment to have my crush close and talking to me. Just the two of us at my favorite spot here against the tree, surrounded by flowers. I really should hate him and yet I'm attracted to his warm eyes and gorgeous face.

"I have something for you," he states and shoves his hand into his pocket to grab something.

My brow furrows and I wonder what he could possibly have for me. It can't be something good, because what on earth could someone give the person they bully? Used to bully? Would he stop now? I snort at my mental ramblings before I start to wonder what Hudson could possibly give the 'freak' of the school.

He suddenly holds a golden card out for me to take. There's a string attached to it so you can wear it around your neck. Strange. I wonder what it's for and mostly, why he's giving it to me.

"What is it?" I question, and tilt my head to the side as I study the card.

A smile appears across his face as he shoves the card in my hands.

"It's a VIP card for my concert tomorrow." His British accent has a thick undertone in his voice when he proudly informs me what the card is supposed to be used for.

"You have a band?" I gasp.

How did I miss that little fact? I thought I stalked him on social media enough to know everything about him. I guess not.

"Yeah, don't you know?" There's honest surprise in his voice and he gives a little shake with his head. "I don't want to brag but, it's pretty popular."

Hudson smirks while I can feel my cheeks heat.

"Sorry." I give him another tiny smile and try not to feel embarrassed or make this moment between us any more awkward than it already is.

I clear my throat and ask, "So what precisely does this card do?"

"If you show this card to the security guys at the concert, you can come in and stand first row. It's really rare to have one of these. That's why I'm giving one to you as a peace offering." He shoots me a wink and I grip the card tighter to keep myself from swooning all over him.

The crush I have is overriding any rational thoughts. I should still be angry at him, at his friends, and shove the card back in his face.

Instead I place the card back into his hand while I get to my feet and tell him, "No way. I can't accept this. It's too expensive. Too special. You'd do best to give this to someone else."

"No. I gave it to you. You're keeping it," Hudson snaps and gets to his feet as well.

He leans in and places his mouth right next to my ear. "I expect to see you tomorrow night. If I don't see you in the crowd, then it would completely ruin my night."

His voice is a mere whisper. Husky, and begging me in that British accent to follow his demand and show up to see him perform. His strong cologne wraps around me and enters my nose as he moves back to stare intently into my eyes. Damn, it's hard to say no when he's this close. Though, I have to stand up for myself. It's not that easy to forgive months of bullying by him, and his pals.

"I'll think about it." I try to keep my voice plain and give him a tight nod.

A smirk slides across his face. He shakes his head as if he needs to clear it before he strolls toward his bike. He gives me one last look as he straddles his bike and fires it up. My belly flips and I take a strand of my hair to wrap it around my finger as I watch him leave.

I guess he's skipping classes, just like I am because there's no way I'm going back inside. My grandparents would be angry if they knew how many classes I've missed already.

My cheeks are still heated from blushing, all because of Hudson with his actions, his words, and mostly…the way he looks at me. I swear I can feel the butterflies flock around inside my stomach trying to break free. It seems that every time I try to dislike Hudson for the things he and his friends do, there's always a moment where I fall right back into adoring him.

No matter how hard I try, my mind and body never allow me to hate him. And I should. I really should for my own sanity. A deep sigh rips from me and I dust off my clothes to get rid of the tiny specks of dirt from sitting on the grass. I wish I could brush away all my problems just as easy.

I throw the cord with the card around my neck and start to walk home, making sure to take my time. My grandma is standing on the porch when I get there, as if she's already expecting me.

"Grandma," I quip and feel a bright smile slide across my face.

"Hey, my sweet girl." She smiles in return and opens her arms.

I dash forward to hug her and feel a wave of happiness inside me. I love coming home; it's where I feel accepted and loved.

"Did you have a good day at school?" she asks and pulls back to watch my face.

I keep my smile in place when I tell her, "Yeah, it was great, grandma."

It's only half a lie because Hudson lightened my mood when he stopped both the bullying and chased me down to give me an apology along with a VIP card to see his band perform.

"What happened to your hoodie?" Grandma frowns when she notices the stains from the food they threw at me.

"It's nothing. I took a detour and went through the forest. I might have caught some branches and smudges or whatever." I shrug in an effort to cover up the truth about what Roan and Steve did.

I don't want my grandparents to find out, they would step up and go to the school and it would only make it worse.

"Okay, well…why don't you give it to me and I'll wash it for you." She holds out her hand.

"Thanks, grandma. I appreciate it." I quickly slide out of the hoodie and hand it to her.

We head inside and she tells me, "There is pasta on the kitchen counter."

I give her a thumbs-up and stalk into the kitchen to snag the bowl from the counter. With my food in hand I jog up the stairs to get to the attic so I can talk to my mother.

"Good evening, Mom," I cheerfully quip and drop myself onto the hardwood floor in front of the mirror, right next to a pillow.

"It took you long enough," my mom says as she appears beside me in the reflection.

The spot she always appears, as if she's sitting on her favorite pillow right beside mine. It's why I always take the spot right next to it on the hardwood floor instead of using the pillow, even if I know she's not really here and can't actually sit on the fluffy thing.

"I know, I had something I needed to do after school," I mutter and take a huge bite of pasta that's still quite hot.

"Oh? Tell me all about it," she eagerly says as she watches how I devour the delicious food grandma made me.

"There is a boy, his name is Hudson. I've told you about him before, right?" I ramble and place the bowl of food on the floor in front of me to let it cool down a bit.

"Seems like an interesting boy if he can make my daughter blush." My mom grins and points at my cheeks, that indeed feel heated by the mere thought of Hudson.

"Mom," I scold and giggle awkwardly.

"Tell me about him. Is he cute?" she asks with a slight tease in her voice.

She knows how shy I am, especially when it comes to boys, and definitely talking about them. She also does this every time I mention someone from school.

To avoid talking about him I hold up the card Hudson gave me and cheerfully quip, "He gave me this."

"Oh. What is it?" She leans forward to get a closer look at the card.

"It's for his concert tomorrow. Apparently he's in a band. It's so cool, he invited me through this personal VIP card. This also gives me access to stand front row, can you believe it?" I gush full of excitement.

"That's awesome, honey. But, please think about the risk you'll be taking when the wrong people find out about your history. Who knows, someone could follow you home and find the flower. I think it's too dangerous to go to this concert," she gently tells me.

"But Mom," I whine and release a deep sigh.

I know she's right, but I'm so excited about the concert and the way Hudson personally invited me. No one ever invites me to anything.

"Maybe it's a trick. You can never be too careful, especially with these things." Her voice is stern.

She doesn't want to hear any excuses or reasons I can think up so she'll agree for me to go. The happiness of getting invited to Hudson's concert quickly fades and all that's left is pain and emptiness. My life is unfair. I get bullied every step I take outside, and when someone finally invites me to do something fun...I can't go because it's too big of a risk.

Mom gets to her feet and places her hands on her hips. "Promise me you won't go."

Her eyes hold mine through the mirror. I can't say no to her, even if she can't do anything if I do decide to go. But it would be wrong and stupid not to listen to her advice. She only wants what's best for me.

"I won't go," I vow.

The words Hudson gave me earlier slip through my mind. 'If I don't see you in the crowd, then it would ruin my day.' I want to go so bad, but I just know the right choice is to listen to my mother.

"Thank you, sweetie. I'm so sorry it has to be this way. But I can't let you risk someone getting close to your heart. You know what happened to me." She releases a deep sigh.

By her pinched expression I can tell she's thinking about what happened to her. My mom is right, it's exactly what happened with her and my dad. Ever since that happened she's overprotective of me and warns me about everything I do and who I hang out with.

I can't blame her, though. She met my dad when she was around my age, then had me when she was around twenty-years-old. Years came and went, and I grew up hearing my parents yell at one another at every turn. They had arguments about the craziest things.

One night a loud scream woke me. I was so scared, but decided to go downstairs and check anyway. I found my mom on the floor and my dad standing over her with the rose in his hands. Blood was dripping through his fingers and splattered to the floor...it came from the rose. He shattered the rose; her heart.

I screamed my lungs out and rushed to my mother's side. My father dropped the rose and left. My mother shared a few words with me to tell me about the rose before she expelled her dying breath.

At the age of thirteen I've been through a lot, and it traumatized me. For years all I could do was hide in my room and cry while my grandparents took care of me. I didn't trust anyone besides them. Until I finally found the strength to pick up my life and go to school.

I wanted to find friends and leave my past behind me. My mom was against the idea, but she knew deep down that I needed it.

"It's okay." I give her a reassuring smile.

It's not her fault that she is so protective of me. She just doesn't want anything bad happening to me. Especially when it comes to trusting someone you like or love and having them taken advantage, which in the end can mean losing your life.

This conversation is getting awkward. I clear my throat. "I should go to bed. It's been a long day and I have school tomorrow."

"Okay, sweets, have a good night's sleep," my mother whispers and disappears.

I reach for the bowl of food and start to eat while I head for my room. It's going to be a long day tomorrow. Placing the bowl on my nightstand, I crash headfirst onto the bed and simply close my eyes.

I might have told my mom that I wouldn't go to the concert, but the truth is…I still haven't made up my mind. I really want to go out and have fun. I deserve to be there and feel alive, even if it's for only a few hours.

It would be extremely selfish of me, and I would be taking a huge risk. But I want to go so badly. For now I'm going to sleep and make my final decision when I wake up tomorrow morning.

A HEART DOOMED BY FATE

CHAPTER 04

HUDSON

I wake up and feel good. It's as if I'm recharged and filled to the brim with energy. Such a drastic change compared to the past few months. To think the only thing different was the fact that I talked to Artsy and gave her a present.

I made her day by giving her the VIP card. The brilliant smile she gave me was a solid reminder. I've never seen a smile like that on her face. I feel damn good about being the one who put it there. Though, I bet Roan and Steve will be pissed when they see her gorgeous face standing first row. But I don't give a shit.

Yawning, I swing my legs off the bed and get to my feet, giving my arms and upper body a good stretch. I turn the alarm off and notice I'm awake twenty minutes early so I have all the time to get ready for school.

I stroll to the closet and grab my school uniform. As usual I add a few items to make it a little more stylish. A necklace, a few bracelets, a couple of chains on my belt and I'm done. Snatching my backpack, I add the books I'll need today and throw it over my shoulder.

Jogging down the stairs, I come face-to-face with my father.

He rubs one of his eyes and says with a groggy voice, "Someone's early."

"You know what day it is, right? I need to be at my best," I grunt.

He waves me off and heads for the kitchen when he throws over his shoulder, "Yeah, yeah. I need coffee to properly function this early. But, good luck today, son."

I chuckle and shake my head as I walk out the door. Straddling my bike, I smile and feel damn good. Firing it up, I guide it onto the road and head to school.

"Ready for our big night?" Roan yells as soon as I've parked my bike.

"Hell yeah, I sure am. After school I'm gonna pick up a few things and meet you guys at the stylist for the appointment we made. Then I'll be all set," I tell him and swing my leg off the bike to give the guy a fist bump.

"Nice, dude," Steve grunts and bumps into my shoulder as he joins the conversation.

"How about you guys? Just as excited?" I ask as the three of us walk inside the school building.

"Totally," they both state in sync.

That's good to hear, this concert might be our best one yet.

"Oh, by the way, Hudson." Roan glances at me with a concerned look on his face.

"What's up?" I frown, wondering what he's concerned about.

He sighs and rubs the back of his neck. "Steve and I haven't come up with any input for a new song to add to the album."

"That's okay." I shrug. "I have one."

They both come to a stop to stare at me. A proud grin slides across my face. Last night the words simply flowed and I've worked on it for a few hours to add the music. I am really proud of how it turned out. It fits perfect in our album.

"No shit?" Steve gasps and keeps staring at me with huge eyes.

"Yeah, really." I nod.

"You're awesome," Roan states and slaps my shoulder.

"We need to go to class, but I'll see you guys later," Steve grunts and walks off to the classroom.

Roan and I continue to stroll down the hall to get to our own classroom.

"I need to get something from my locker. I'll see you in class, Roan," I tell him.

He gives me a thumbs-up and wanders off. I turn and jog in the direction of my locker. I don't want to be late for class three days in a row. That would be a little bit too embarrassing, and I don't think they'll let me slip by with a mere warning this time.

I slide my fingers over the lock to enter my code and it pops open. Snatching my water bottle out of my locker, I check the time. Shit. I'm late. Even if I jump into a run I won't make it to class. So much for being on time for once.

I release a deep sigh and take my time since it won't matter anyway. I stroll toward class, completely annoyed. Before I open the door, I shoot a quick look inside. I notice Roan laughing with a few friends. Glancing over the rest to find Artsy, I come up empty. Where is she? She's always on time. Roan and Steve are both in their classroom so it can't be them holding her up.

I grit my teeth at the thought and glance down the hallway at the exit. "Screw it," I mutter and turn around to jog through the hallway.

Once I open the door and step outside I instantly glance in the direction of where she's always sitting in the field of flowers. Nothing. She isn't sitting against the tree. Where the hell is she? Is she sitting somewhere else? Simply staying home and skipping class?

I stalk toward the tree. Maybe she's skipping class to study for something? Somehow I need to know if she's okay. I always notice her. If she's sitting quietly in class, ignoring everyone while moving through the hallways, silently crying in a corner, or like always, sitting against the tree.

She's intriguing, an enigma. Though, now my brain is triggered by worry. Is she not in class because of me or my friends? Does she feel forced to come to my concert tonight, afraid we'll do worse if she doesn't show up? Maybe wondering if we'd do something to her during the concert? I didn't mean to cause her worries.

A deep sigh rips from me and I drop myself in the field of flowers with my back against the tree. I close my eyes and I enjoy the feeling of the wind brushing against my skin and through my messy hair. I forgot to tame it with a brush this morning.

"Artsy, where are you," I murmur to myself.

The realization of everything makes me feel bad for her. It's all my fault. I've been the one who bullied her. Not just my friends; I've been an active part in it as well. I remember every single incident because I've always noticed her. Maybe that's why I teased her the first time. How teasing became bullying over time, I really have no idea.

Though, that's what it came to and now that it escalated due to my friends getting physical…maybe that's what opened my eyes? I don't know, but I feel sick sitting here and realizing how much it affected her. Hell, I might not even know what goes on in that pretty head of her, though it's not hard to figure out how much my words, my actions, can hurt…have hurt her.

Shit. Why am I getting sentimental and suddenly confronted by all these feelings? Is the tree I'm leaning against cursed or something? One day I'm bullying her, the next I feel bad for her.

When I woke up this morning I was excited and happy. Hell, last night I wrote a new song while inspiration has been lacking for a while now. Yet, seeing my friends hurting Artsy, knowing their actions are wrong and going past the whole 'degrade others 'cause we're the popular kids' confronted me with the reality of it all.

I shake my head and relish in the quiet moment where there's only nature surrounding me. Birds chirping, wind blowing, a clear blue sky above me and the sun warming my skin. Now I understand why Artsy likes this place. It's soothing and makes you forget about everything, even time.

I'm ripped out of my moment when my phone starts to ring and vibrate inside my pocket. Shoving my hand in my pocket, I fish my phone out and glance at the screen to see who's calling me. It's Roan.

I yawn when I hear Roan grumble, "Dude, where are you? You said you were gonna grab something from your locker, not stay gone for hours."

"Calm down. I went outside for some fresh air and time simply slipped away from me," I tell him with a groggy voice.

"Time slipped away? How does that even happen? You know what? It really doesn't matter. Just come to the stylist. We have an appointment, remember? We're all waiting for you," he snaps and hangs up before I can reply.

"What time is it?" I mutter to myself. "There's no way I've been sitting here for…shit."

Really? Hours? I fell asleep and slept for hours against this tree? Damn, I can definitely vouch for this place having a calming effect. No wonder the girl sits here to forget about her problems to get some peace and quiet, making time flash by.

I get to my feet and brush away the specks of dirt clinging to my pants. It doesn't matter if my clothes are dirty because I'm heading to the stylist and I have to change for the concert anyway.

Skipping class and sitting in this place to gather my thoughts has done me some good. Not to mention, last night as well when I wrote that song and woke up completely recharged. Tonight will be awesome. The fans will go crazy when they hear the new song.

I jog to my bike and straddle it. We're gonna need all the time we can get to rehearse the new song. First things first. The stylist. We only have a few more hours before the concert. I ride to the building where the others are and park in front of it.

"There you are," Steve grumbles when I step inside the stylist's shop.

"Yeah, yeah. I know I'm late. Let's get this over with and we can chat later," I tell him and we all take a seat in the three free chairs.

"Sorry I'm late, but I'm here now," I tell the stylist.

The woman has been helping us each time we have a concert. Not just with our appearance, but also by giving all of us a haircut.

"No worries. We still have enough time for all of you." She gives me a polite smile.

The woman works on my hair while I sit in the chair for over an hour. It's a messy hair look with some wet shine to it. The fans seem to like it and I'm fine with whatever. Roan has his hair curled, and Steve's hair is slicked back into a ponytail. The woman applies some cream and makeup, or whatever she applies to our faces, and then it's time to put on our clothes.

"Follow me," the woman quips and we stroll after her into a room where three outfits are already laid out for us.

I blink a few times to process how perfect the outfit she picked for me is. It resembles the style of our album perfectly.

"Hudson," she says when she points at my outfit. "This is your look for tonight."

I grin and greedily accept it to head for the changing room. Stepping inside, I close the door and change into a pair of grey ripped jeans with loads of chains hanging from the side. I shrug on a white tank top along with it and I'm glad for it because I always get hot during the concert.

I stare in the mirror and even if the look is good with the hair and the pants, I feel like I'm missing something crucial.

There's a knock on the door and I hear the stylist quip, "Hudson? You forgot something."

I open the door for her and she hands me a leather vest. "This is also for you."

She leaves to check on the others and I stare down at the leather vest with embroided details and shiny stones attached to the front of it.

"Woah. Nice," I rumble.

I turn the vest to look at the back. My eyes go wide when I notice the rose on the back. The rose looks so vivid and special. It is a black rose with red lines crossing the petals. The rose is surrounded by a white line so it really makes it pop with the black of the leather vest.

I can't wait to put it on. Turning to the mirror I shove my arms through the holes and stare at my perfect outfit for tonight. Grinning, I step out of the changing room to meet the others.

"What do you think?" I rumble when I see Roan and Steve.

"That's a damn fine choice. For all of us," Steve says, giving the stylist a compliment.

"I love it. And I'm sure the fans will cheer extra loud tonight. They love seeing you in leather," Roan states with a little smirk on his face.

"Too bad most won't see the cool lines in the rose on the back. Well, they would if you'd turn your back to the audience." Steve chuckles.

He's right, I love the rose on the back, but most won't be able to notice it, or all the details it holds. It doesn't make it any less cool, though. I still love the leather vest.

"You can keep the vest," the stylist tells me and jerks her chin at the others when she adds, "All the other stuff as well."

"No way! Thanks." I give her a huge grin.

"No thanks needed. You guys mention us as a sponsor so I consider it free advertising." She shoots Roan a wink.

We all thank her again and grab our stuff so we can get out of there. Just a little while longer and then it's time for the concert. At least our clothes show we're ready for it. Roan is wearing black jeans and when the lights hit the fabric it shows a hint of glitter at every turn. He has a fire-engine-red tank top above it. Steve is wearing the same jeans as Roan but instead of a red tank top, he's wearing a grey one with added chains across it. All of us are wearing our biker boots.

"Let's head over to the venue, shall we? Then we can get everything ready and rehearse the new tune," Roan suggests as he zips up his leather jacket.

"Alright," Steve grunts and I nod in agreement.

And that's exactly what we do; pack our stuff and leave the stylist to get ready for the concert.

ARTSY

"What are you still doing in your bed?" My grandma's voice rips me from my sleep and I have to blink a few times before I realize she's standing in my room.

"What's wrong?" I ask, panic hitting me full force.

"It's five in the afternoon. What are you still doing in bed? Did you even go to school?" my grandma asks, worry clear in her tone of voice.

"Five? That can't be right. Are you sure?" I ask, shocked to hear what time it is.

There is no way I slept all through the day. Even if it took me hours to eventually fall asleep last night. Besides, I never forget to set my alarm. This can't be happening. One glance at the clock proves otherwise. Shit. I'm so stupid. I completely skipped school, and now I'm bound to miss the concert.

"I'm so sorry, grandma," I tell her and yawn.

"It's okay. You must have needed the sleep. There is dinner downstairs if you're hungry. Get dressed and we'll chat some more," she says and leaves the room.

I sure am lucky to have my grandmother react this way instead of flipping out. Getting to my feet, I stretch my arms and roll my shoulders. Last night I tossed and turned, my mind going a hundred miles an hour with all the thoughts going through it. I still haven't decided if I should go to the concert or not.

I really want to because I want to see Hudson. Especially when it was he who gave me the VIP card to come see him. So, I guess I have made up my mind about going to the concert. I glance at the clock again and realize I should hurry up.

The concert starts in a few hours and I need to get dressed, go downstairs to get something to eat, talk to grams, and do my makeup and my hair. Oh, and let's not forget, I still have to get to the venue to be there on time.

I wander to the closet and glance over everything to pick a good-looking outfit. Everything seems plain and nothing feels right. Shit. I have no nice clothes to wear for a night out. I sigh but suddenly realize I might still have something that used to be my mom's.

My grandma put all my mother's clothes in a box after she passed away and kept it in the attic. There's only one problem with going up to the attic; the mirror is there. I can't look in it or my mother will appear with my reflection and she will see me stealing a dress. She will instantly know it's for the concert.

So, I sneak upstairs and try not to look at any smooth surface that will show my reflection. The box with my mother's clothes is easy to find, and there are so many clothes inside. I glance through everything until something catches my interest. After a few minutes I pull a red fabric from of the box. It is sparkling and very soft. I love it, and it's definitely the dress I want to wear tonight.

Closing the box, I rush down the stairs to my room where I hold the dress up to stare at it. The fabric is a stunning cherry red lace combined with some glitter. It looks absolutely stunning.

"This is it," I proudly state and feel a grin sliding across my face.

Throwing the dress on the bed, I head downstairs and meet my grandparents in the kitchen. I try to rush dinner, but don't want to seem too eager to leave. We make some small talk and then I'm finally able to slip away and return to my room to get ready for the concert.

I hop into the bathroom to take a quick shower. Once done I slip into the dress and it fits perfectly around my body, like it was made for me. Such a shame I can't check myself in the mirror; I simply can't risk giving my mother a chance to slip into my reflection.

Snatching a hair tie off my desk, I braid the top part of my hair and leave the rest down and curl it. I've taught myself to apply makeup without the use of a mirror and that's why I easily add a hint of eyeshadow and mascara before I apply some lipstick that matches the color of my dress.

To make my look complete I add a necklace along with some bracelets and slide into my red heels. I bought them online two years ago, even though I never had a reason to wear them. I just thought they were cute and I guess it's meant to be because now I get to wear them for the first time.

I take my purse and put my phone in there. I slide the chain of the purse over my shoulder and am about to sneak down the stairs when I realize I also need the ticket. I quickly shove the VIP card in there as well and silently make my way downstairs. I hear my grandparents chatting in the living room and manage to tiptoe out the backdoor. Part one of my mission completed!

As I walk around the house and get to the street, I find a car with a driver parked alongside the street. How strange.

The driver opens the door and frowns as he takes in my dress. "Are you Artsy by any chance?"

"Yeah, that's me." I give him a timid smile and wonder how he knows my name and why he's sitting in front of my grandparents' house. That can't be a coincidence.

He opens the door to the backseat and says, "Hudson asked me to pick you up. He gave me instructions to bring you to his concert. I've been waiting for about twenty minutes for you to show up. Hop in."

Oh my goodness. Hudson did this for me? My chest fills with warmth. That's so sweet of him. Such a gentleman.

"Thanks. I appreciate it," I tell him and slide into the backseat, excited about the fact that I'm going to make it to the concert before it starts.

The drive doesn't take too long. The driver parks right in front of the venue and steps out to open the door for me. This is it. My smile is huge as I walk to the door.

A tall man in a suit stops me and asks, "Miss. Where do you think you're going?" He frowns and glances at my empty hands. "Do you have a ticket?"

"Oops. Yes, here," I ramble and open my purse to take out the VIP card and slide it around my neck.

"Perfect, miss. Now you go and have a good time," he says and steps aside to allow me access to the venue.

I step inside a large room with different colored lights flickering around me. I gasp in awe, this is so cool.

"Follow me," a man states when he notices the card around my neck.

He's wearing the same suit as the security guy at the door. I nod, even if the guy has already given me his back as he leads me through the crowd until we're standing front row. I can't wait to see Hudson walk onstage.

If I'm being honest, I have to admit that I'm getting a bit claustrophobic standing here. There's a huge crowd behind me, people left and right, and I'm tightly pressed against a fence that separates the stage from the crowd. Everyone wants to get as close as they can to the band.

"Hudson!" I hear someone scream from behind me.

The room plunges into darkness and spotlights are turned on left and right, focusing on the stage. Oh, I think it's starting. I glance up to the stage and at that very moment Hudson strolls in as if he owns the place.

He's standing there in ripped, gray jeans and a tight white tank top covered by a leather vest. His hair is styled with a wild look that fits his personality perfectly. I think he's never looked as attractive as he does right now. Everyone around me screams his name. Jeez, I won't be surprised if I've lost some of my hearing when I leave this place.

"Welcome, everybody." His voice rings loud through the crowd, heavy with his British accent.

I could listen to him talk forever and can't wait to hear him use that voice to sing. He's standing in front of the microphone when he glances around as if he's looking for someone. The crowd is quiet, waiting patiently for him to start singing.

"There you are," Hudson murmurs with a cocky grin right into the microphone to let everyone know he found what he's looking for.

Me. He's looking right at me. An "Ooooh" flows through the room from the people surrounding me who realize the lead singer of this band is staring at a girl. I can feel my cheeks heat while my stomach flips. My whole body becomes aware of his intense stare.

"Let's start our first song, shall we?" he states and shakes his head, as if he needs to clear it and focus on what he came here to do.

The crowd cheers loudly in reply. Their songs sound amazing, one after the other, and even if I never heard any of them before today, I enjoy myself immensely. The people around me loudly sing along with the lyrics of some songs.

Time flies by until Hudson suddenly says, "Sadly, we've come to the last song and then we have to call it a night, folks."

His British accent makes the room fall silent and I stare in awe how Hudson looks at ease on the stage, as if he belongs there. The way he handles himself, the crowd, the tunes, his singing voice, it all amazes me.

"But, like you all know, we have one last surprise left. The reason why all of you are here," he states and all the people break out in a wave of applause.

I have no idea what they are talking about, but it sounds enthralling and he sure has everyone's attention.

"We finished some new stuff for our upcoming album and tonight we're going to treat you guys with one song. Before we start, I would like to say something about this new song I wrote."

He releases a deep sigh and takes the microphone off the stand. He wanders over to the edge of the stage and sits down. He's so close. If I stretch my arm out I would be able to touch him.

"This song is for a special girl. I know, I know, most songs are, but I would lie if I didn't admit that this song was inspired by a very special girl," Hudson starts and wipes his sweaty wet hair out of his face.

Everyone is hanging on his every word falling from his lips, waiting patiently and curious to hear what this song is all about. Hell, maybe they're all nosey and want to know who this special girl is because it could be anyone.

"Every single day when I go to my bike after class, I see this girl sitting against a tree surrounded by flowers. Her hair lights up like gold in the sun and she has the prettiest lime green eyes. I never understood the peace someone could find just by sitting or reading a book somewhere. But doing it myself today? I now realize it actually changes a lot." His eyes slide to me.

Wait, is he talking about me?

I can feel the emotion course through my veins, causing my cheeks to flush and my eyes start to water. Not once did it cross my mind it would be me who inspired Hudson. He's a bully I have a stupid crush on.

He never led me to believe he'd noticed me otherwise. I always just thought he only noticed me long enough to make fun of me.

"So, this song is for her." He shoots me a wink and jumps back to his feet.

His two bandmates and friends glare at him and I'm fairly sure they had no idea about Hudson's admittance just now. The song starts and I'm completely captivated by the lyrics and tunes. When the last line flows through the venue, I'm an emotional mess.

My vision is blurry due to the tears and my throat hurts from trying to keep my emotions to myself. All of this aside I'm also filled with joy and happiness and there's a huge smile across my face. I can't believe this happened. This night, this moment.

"Thank you, Artsy," Hudson's husky voice teases my ears as I hear my name on his tongue.

Hudson doesn't care that he's acknowledging me in front of a whole crowd. Not even caring about his two friends and bandmates who are still glaring daggers at him. Hudson might not have stood up for me before, and bullied me as well...but something sure has changed now.

The shock of it all hits me hard and I suddenly feel completely drained. The yelling and screaming is still going strong around me. I close my eyes for a brief moment and tip my head back. When I open them I notice the ceiling is filled with mirrors.

Why didn't I notice this before? I stare at my reflection and it's then I see my mom standing behind me with an angry look in her eyes. Dammit. Why mirrors? Why couldn't I be more careful to hide my reflection? Now it's all ruined and she found out I went to the concert even if she warned me not to.

I drop my head and glance behind me at the row of people. I have to get out of here.

"Excuse me," I mutter as I worm myself through all the bodies.

I need fresh air. I have to get out of here. Once I step out I feel the rain hitting my skin. It's freezing in this dress and my feet are hurting from standing on my new heels all night. Why didn't I bring a coat? I wipe at my wet face. I knew this was a dumb idea.

Whirling around I ask the bouncer at the door, "Is there a taxi somewhere? Can you call one for me?"

He shakes his head and sighs. "No, ma'am. Sorry."

I feel new tears well in my eyes. Why can't anything go right for a change? I seem to ruin everything for myself no matter what I do. A bad decision to go to school, if I didn't? Nothing would have happened. No bullying, no meeting Hudson, no stupid concert, and no standing alone in the rain without a ride home.

"Fine," I snap to no one in particular, unable to keep my emotions inside. "I'll freaking walk home, see if I care."

"That's not going to happen," a voice coming from behind me snaps and at the same time I feel a strong arm wrap around my waist to pull me against a strong body.

"Let me go," I yell, and struggle to turn in this person's grip.

I try to elbow the person in the face but when I catch a glimpse of blond hair along with the cyan eyes staring at me, I realize it's Hudson holding me.

"Hudson," I gasp.

What is he doing here? He was still standing onstage when I left. Shouldn't he...I don't know...wrap up the concert or something?

"I'm leaving," I grumble and yet again try to release myself from his grip.

I don't want to keep him from whatever it is he needs to do after a concert.

"No way. Did I do something wrong? Was the song too much? My speech before I sang the song? Do you hate me or something? I mean, I'd totally understand if you do, Artsy. I've been such a prick to you. You're absolutely right to walk away from me. I'm sorry. I truly am," he rattles, his voice strained with emotion.

He sounds torn, as if he's going to burst into tears at any second. There's truth to his words, the song, his admittance…what does it all even mean? I turn and this time he lets me go so I can stare at him.

Rain continues to fall down on us when I tell him, "I didn't walk away because of you, or due to the speech, or the song for that matter. I promise."

Stepping closer I place a hand on his chest and feel his breath hitch under my palm.

"You didn't?" he whispers. "Then why are you standing outside in the rain, wanting to leave instead of inside waiting for me to come get you so we can go backstage together?"

I wish I could tell him the truth, that I didn't have to hide anything from him. Sadly, I can't tell him how my mother warned me not to go. How she appears behind me whenever I see my own reflection. It would be too big of a risk. Not just for myself, the flower in the attic, or any of it…but he would be questioning my sanity…he'd never believe me.

So, instead I tell him, "You wouldn't understand."

"Then explain it to me. Make me understand by giving me all the details, all your worries, all your fears. I'm here for you, I promise." His words hit my heart and cause a fire inside me that's heated by adoration.

This guy. How can he give me all the right words? Capture me with his intense stare, and go from my bully who I have a crush on to the guy I'm breaking my mother's promises for just to be with him?

He slides his leather vest off and I catch a brief glimpse of the back before he throws it over my shoulders. "Here. It's freezing cold in the rain and you're only wearing a dress. I don't want you to get sick."

"Wait a second." I gasp, my mind barely processing the image on the back of his leather vest.

A rose. A black rose with red lines crossing the petals. The one I have. The one my mother explained about.

"A dark rose with blood lines pumping through it. It's like your heart

blooming on the outside," my mother's voice and words slide through my head.

It's the exact same flower embroidered on Hudson's leather vest. How is that even remotely possible? No one knows about it, expect my family.

CHAPTER 06

HUDSON

"What?" I wonder, noticing the surprise in her eyes as she stares at the leather vest.

Is there something wrong with it? It might be a little damp. I can't help it, I wore it all night onstage and it gets hot up there.

"Here, just take it. You're shaking from the rain and the cold." I ignore her staring and wrap the leather over her shoulders. "There you go."

I give her a smile and she mindlessly nods, as if she's still processing the way I offered her my leather cut, or the way it looks, whatever.

"Thanks." Her voice sounds strange, distant, as if she's confused about something.

I have so many questions burning inside me, wanting to soothe my curiosity when it comes to this girl. Though, I have to keep my cool and stay focused. She almost ran off without giving me a chance to catch up and talk to her.

"So, why did you leave before we had a chance to talk?" I question her once more. "If it's my fault, you can say it to my face, I promise I'll understand. I also promise I won't get mad. We've moved past that. I'd never do anything to hurt you. Never again," I fiercely tell her.

We stare into one another's eyes, raindrops are sliding down her face. She's so damn gorgeous.

"It's not your fault. I love the song, I adored your speech, it was very touching, and I adore–" she abruptly shuts her mouth to swallow the rest of her words.

"What was that last part?" I frown and try to get her to finish her sentence.

"No. It was nothing. I liked it. Everything. Thanks for the song. I'm glad I inspired you to write it and that you learned from it," she quickly rattles.

Somehow I'm triggered to find out what she was going to say. The way she rattled to cover up her reaction is just a bit too suspicious. There's something going on. First her reaction to my leather vest, and now this.

"Artsy." I gently place my hand on her arm to gain her full attention. "I don't have an excuse for the times I've bullied you, other than the fact that I didn't realize the effect it had on you. Me and the guys were just shooting the shit, having fun. Yeah, it was at your expense and I realize that now. Well, only after they went too far with their actions. They physically hurt you. And I know it's just as bad as the mental shit. I'm sorry for my part in all of it."

I release a deep sigh and decide to open up. "When I noticed you weren't at school today, my chest tightened with worry. I even went to the spot where you are always sitting against the tree. You weren't there and I took your spot instead. It made me think and realize that you are worth confronting my friends and standing up for…to fight for you."

My heart is beating in my throat as nervousness fills my veins. I never open myself up to anyone. It's an action set for failure that'll give people fuel to start shit whenever they want to hurt you in return.

It's driving me crazy that she just stares at me and hasn't said a word yet. Why is she staying quiet? Everything I said was the truth. Was I not clear enough?

I rub the back of my neck and decide to add, "Sure, I'm scared of losing my friends, my bandmates over this. But, Artsy? You're actually the one I want to be around. I want to get to know you, talk some more, hang out. You…you make me want to do better…be the better person…I guess."

She blinks a few times and nibbles on her bottom lip, drawing my attention to her mouth. My mind jumps at the thought to kiss her, but now is not the time.

Shit. I can't stand the silence and I guess it's why I keep rambling. "I can't keep my eyes off you. I never realized how I felt until someone hurt you. I couldn't stand watching you in pain. The protectiveness I feel when it comes to you is real, and I want to explore exactly what this connection is between us."

Now I'm the one biting my lip before I start rambling about romantic shit. Though, it's better for her to know where I stand before we explore whatever it is between us. One thing I do know, and that's the fact that I don't want her to hate me or see me as her bully. I want to stand beside her, be friends...be...I don't know, more?

I can't begin to imagine what Roan and Steve would think if they heard anything of what I just told her. But, I don't care. She is the only one who matters.

I stay silent and take in her expression in the hope to get an impression of how my words might affect her. The rain continues to soak our clothes and I'm freezing, standing here in just my tank top.

She steps closer and murmurs, "I might regret this."

I have no clue what she means by this statement until she places her hands on my shoulders and pushes herself on her tiptoes. The distance between our lips evaporates and a jolt of electricity hits my body when her mouth touches mine.

Instinctively I reach out to cup the back of her head, tilting it slightly to the side to deepen the kiss. Talk about pure chemistry. The kind people write songs about. I now understand the true meaning behind some of my favorite lyrics.

The kiss ends way too soon and it has completely caught me off guard.

Chuckling I whisper, "Woah."

"What?" She gives me a shy smile and wipes the rain off her cheeks.

"I was unsure how you'd react, but I sure as hell didn't expect that," I reply with a huge grin on my face.

"Hudson?" I hear someone snap from behind me.

I whirl around and notice both Roan and Steve standing side by side in front of the building. Their faces a mask of shock and disgust.

"First you're skipping class to search for her, then the new song, and now this?" Roan growls and points an accusing finger at Artsy.

"I knew he wasn't one of us. He is just like her, useless trash. You guys belong together," Steve snaps, anger clearly written all over his face.

"It's not like that," I bark at the two idiots.

Why the hell are they overreacting? I know how badly they have treated Artsy. But they are still my friends, my band members. I don't have to explain myself or my reactions to them, and I can surely decide who I can or can't hang out with. Does our friendship mean nothing to them?

"Then why did you kiss her, eh?" Steve asks with an evil smirk, knowing I can't deny my actions.

I turn back to face the girl who just blew my mind with the kiss she gave me. Her eyes are filled with hurt from the words I just gave my so-called friends.

"I didn't mean it," I whisper and reach for her in an effort to soothe her, and the ache in my chest I feel.

"Yeah, right. Save the bullshit for your friends. I don't want to see you anymore," she snaps and slowly backs away from me.

Her words render me speechless. I can hear Steve and Roan whisper and laugh behind me.

"Please, Artsy," I try once more.

I step forward to stop her from leaving but she shakes her head and runs off.

"Artsy!" I yell.

She can't just leave like this. It's dark, the middle of the night, rain is pouring down and there might just be a storm brewing. No taxi in sight. How the hell is she going to get home on foot, all by herself?

"Whoops, there she goes." Steve chuckles, shamelessly enjoying the scene in front of him.

I whirl around to face them and growl, "You two."

"Ruh-roh, I think we made him mad," Roan fake whispers to Steve.

Rage rushes through my body. I never thought I would do this, not at this point, and certainly not after we gave one hell of a concert just now, but it has to be done. "Screw the both of you, I'm out. From this moment on I'm going solo. That's if I ever decide to get up on a stage again."

"What? You can't do that," Roan growls.

Steve stares at me with wide eyes. "That's crazy. You need us."

As much as I want to take the words back, I simply can't. There's no forgetting what just happened and there's no way I can justify the way they treat Artsy, or me for hanging out with her for that matter. We make music about love, about friendship and trust. With what they just did? These two showed that they don't know shit about those values in life and lack any kind of respect.

I release a deep sigh and want to say something to them, but nothing comes to mind. I can't do this. I simply don't care about anything else than going after the girl who yet again received the short end of the stick in all of it. Spinning around, I turn my back on my friends as I jog in the direction Artsy disappeared in.

I hope I can find her, she can't have gone that far. I run down the streets, my clothes soaking wet, and yet there's still no trace of Artsy. Why is it so hard to find her? This would be so much easier if I had my motorcycle. Sighing in frustration, I might as well give up and go home. I have no clue where she lives and I don't know in which direction she ran off in.

My pace changes from a jog into a stroll as I go around the corner. Movement catches my attention and I notice a glimpse of red. A door opens and I clearly see the back of my leather vest before it disappears into a house. It's Artsy!

I rush toward the house and raise my hand to knock on the door. Would she let me in? Will she still be angry with me? Should I give her some space and come back in the morning? Screw it. Enough thinking. Here goes nothing.

A HEART DOOMED BY FATE

CHAPTER 07

ARTSY

I kick my heels off to relieve the pain in my feet the second I enter the house. A relieved sigh flows from me as I shut the door behind me. Almost instantly I hear a knock and wonder if I might have dropped something that a neighbor noticed or something like that. I mean, there's no way my grandparents ordered food at this time, and it's too late for someone to swing by for a visit.

I don't feel like opening the door, but I guess I have to in case there's an emergency or something. I reluctantly open the door and come face to face with the person who causes emotional turmoil inside me. One I just ran away from and hoped to never see again.

There's no stopping the rage, sadness, pain, happiness, adoration… too many feelings and emotions to handle that fill my veins at the sight of a drenched Hudson standing on my grandparents' doorstep.

"Hudson." I swallow hard when his cyan eyes collide with mine.

Raindrops slide over his skin, and he's standing there, soaking wet in just his jeans and tank.

I frown. "Did you follow me all the way to my house?"

"I know it's creepy, and I probably shouldn't have done it, but I had to know you got home safe," he murmurs slightly out of breath, as if he's been running the whole way.

Did he? I didn't think I'd meant anything to him the way he acted after his friends caught us. Maybe it's a trick? And why should I even bother to talk to him? This is never going to work between us.

Though, I would like to know. "Why?"

"Because, Artsy, I care about you. They caught me off guard, and I reacted poorly," he says with a load of regret in his voice.

I fidget with my fingers behind my back. I have no idea what to say to that. Should I simply forgive him? Slam the door in his face? We do have a history between us, one that involves his friends as well and it's quite the turnaround between me and Hudson. No matter how big my crush is on him, I do have to protect myself, and my heart. Especially when the kiss we shared felt so special.

He steps closer. "Look, I know I screwed up. And I totally understand your reaction. But I can't walk away from you, Artsy. You're special. That kiss...I just...please, Artsy."

"I don't know," I whisper, unsure of myself and the whole situation.

My eyes stray to the floor and I'm holding onto the door as if I'm ready to close it any second.

"I think it would be best if you went home," I croak and slowly close the door.

In one smooth movement he steps forward and pushes the door wide open. "I'm sorry, Artsy."

The words are loaded with regret and the open and honest look in his eyes gives me the acknowledgement that his apology is real. He mentioned before how he never says those words and for him to give them to me now is still unbelievable.

"What?" I shake my head trying to wrap my brain around this situation.

"You heard me, Artsy. I am sorry for my actions. Everything in our past and especially what happened just now with my so-called friends. I don't want you to be mad at me. That just doesn't feel right to me," he admits.

The statement he just gave me sounds surreal. He's shivering from the cold and is soaking wet.

I take a step back and tell him, "Why don't you come in? You must be so cold from the rain."

He stares at me with wide eyes as he takes in my offer.

"I mean it." I smile. "I could make us some hot cocoa to warm up."

He nods and fully enters the house. I close the door behind him and we both wander into the living room. My grandma looks up from where she sits on the couch. She scans Hudson from head to toe.

"Who are you?" she demands with a confused look on her face.

Luckily she doesn't question me about my appearance and I quickly tell her, "Sorry, I invited him. It's cold outside and it's raining. Hudson just came from a concert. He is in my class and I told him he could crash here. If that's okay with you guys of course."

I soften my face into a pleading one, hoping she doesn't kick him out.

"Fine. Just for tonight." She nods and turns back to watching the tv.

I glance at Hudson who is already looking at me.

"Let's go upstairs and get you some dry clothes," I murmur and turn to jog up the stairs.

"No weird stuff, kids!" my grandma yells after us.

My cheeks heat in embarrassment and I give myself a facepalm while Hudson doesn't seem to mind because the guy just chuckles.

"Go wait in my room, I'll grab you some clothes," I tell him and point at the open door to my room.

I dash into the bedroom that belongs to my grandparents and take a pair of sweatpants and an old t-shirt from my grandfather to make sure they will fit Hudson. My mind is still a mess with doubts about me doing the right thing for letting him in again.

On the other hand, he did run after me, is soaking wet, apologized, and wouldn't take no for an answer. I should give him the benefit of the doubt and I guess only time will tell if he's truly involved the way he says he is.

"I got you the clothes." I hold up the pile in my hands.

Hudson is standing near my desk and is holding a picture in his hand. I drop the clothes and snatch the photograph from his fingers.

"What are you doing?" I demand in a harsh tone.

"Woah. Calm down, princess." Hudson smirks and holds his hands palms up in surrender.

"You can't just enter my room and sneak through my personal stuff," I snap and hold the photograph tightly against my chest.

"You're right. I'm sorry for snooping."

Another apology, one that comes fast and easy this time. I hope he actually means them.

I quickly place the photograph into one of the drawers of my desk. It's a picture taken by my grandma. It's of me and my mom standing by a field of flowers while she's holding the black rose with red veins covering the petals. It is my rose; my heart. He can't see that picture, it's private and it should stay a secret. He can never find out about it, about me, about my family.

He clears his throat, breaking the awkward silence between us while he says, "So, you found some clothes for me?"

"Yeah, you should change before you create a puddle on the carpet," I joke and stroll back to where I dropped the clothes to hand them to him.

He nods. "Thanks. So, where can I change?"

"Bathroom." I point at the door across from my room.

"Thanks. I'll be quick," he tells me and leaves.

Great. Now all I have to do is survive the night with him. I'm still not sure I forgive him, or know how to go from here. I do know I couldn't leave him standing on the doorstep or slam the door in his face without talking some more.

I face the desk that has a mirror in front of it. When I glance at it I don't see my reflection or my mother for that matter. No. It fills with an image of the attic, as if it's showing me something to warn me.

Hudson is in the attic. Fear hits me hard when I see him staring at the flower as he closes the distance between it. Shit. Why did I let him into the house? Why didn't I think of the risks of him going upstairs? I'm so stupid. And why isn't he changing into dry clothes in the bathroom but went straight to the attic instead? It doesn't make sense.

The fear becomes real when I watch in the mirror how Hudson takes the protection away around the rose. He now has the opportunity to reach for it with his hands. He can destroy it, my heart…destroy me…at any second.

Is this even real or is the mirror playing tricks with me? Shit. What am I thinking? I have to check to make sure. I whirl around and rush out of my room to head for the attic. I feel wetness coming from my eyes. Am I crying?

Swiping my fingers over my cheek, I pull my hand back and it's covered with crimson. Blood is dripping from my eyes? What the hell is going on? My heart is racing as I race up the stairs. I have to stop this; I have to stop him, before it's too late.

Out of breath I push the door open and enter the attic. Hudson is standing near the table and has my rose in his hand. His eyes hold mine and are filled with pure anger while mine are filled with desperation. He looks so evil and nothing like the Hudson I know, the one I talked to mere minutes ago.

"Put it back," I snap, my voice carrying a hint of fear and desperation while the blood continues to drip from my eyes, over my cheeks, and is now staining my chest.

"I can't," he answers in weird dark voice.

That isn't Hudson talking. It can't be. It's as if there's an undertone that's a hint of Hudson's voice, but the harsh and dark voice? Not his. Almost like…no. He can't be possessed, right? That's not possible.

Okay, the whole 'that rose is my heart' thing might be mind-blowing and not normal, but really? Possession?

"Hudson?" my voice shakes.

He has a menacing look on his face. One I've never seen him give me, even when he was bullying me, he never truly showed me an evil side. Hell, he stood up to his friends more than once. Why is he doing this? I'm close to freaking out. He can't be the monster he appears to be. Though, he is holding the rose, my heart, in his hand…my life is in his hands…and the look he gives me shows I might not survive this.

He's clutching the rose tightly, the thorns are biting into his skin. There is blood dripping through his fingers and splashing onto the floor. I can feel my chest getting tighter, making it difficult to breathe.

"Please. Don't do this to me," I croak and stumble forward in an effort to make him see that I'm begging for my life.

"I need to do this," he replies with a slightly different tone and his hand starts to shake but then his grip becomes firm again.

"No. No, you don't." I swallow hard, terrified for this moment.

My mother tried to warn me, the first time after it happened to her, and every other time when I spoke to her reflection. I failed her, and myself. This is all on me, I let Hudson into the house, I opened up to him. My mother specifically told me to never trust anyone…the one time I did this happens. She was right and now I have to pay for it with my life.

"You know I do because you don't belong here," he shouts in a completely different voice.

He tightens the grip on the rose some more and I clutch my chest as the blood coming from my eyes intensifies. I can feel it streaming down my face and it's hard to catch my breath. My knees are wobbly as I step closer.

"What do you mean? I don't understand." It's hard to push the words over my lips when my chest burns and feels as if it's being crushed.

I stumble and my knees give out, making me crumble to the floor.

"People like you don't have a right to live. Witches need to burn. That's your destiny, to rot in hell for an eternity. Just the way your mother died, only now it's your turn. Do you remember that, little Artsy? When you woke up from the screaming of your dying mother, watching the rose crumble and her life along with it? Yes, you do, don't you? That's how your kind deserves to die."

His words terrify me. Not only did he crush me by tightening his grip on the rose, but he is literally ripping me apart from the inside out by these memories. Flashbacks from the day I found my mother hit me hard and it's exactly the way he just described. He is right, this is what happened to my mom, and now it's my destiny as well?

Anger wells up inside me and I snap, "My mom was a good person. She didn't deserve what happened to her."

She never hurt another person and was always sweet and loving. To me, and to everyone else. I miss her so much. How could someone take her life in such a gruesome way? Exactly what I'm experiencing right now as well as I scream when more pain rips through me from the inside out.

CHAPTER 08

ARTSY

"You think? Why do you think people like you exist?" he huffs and rips a petal off the rose.

I feel a sharp stabbing pain burning through my heart. A scream rips from my lips while all he does is smile.

It's hard to take a breath and push out the words, but I don't understand his anger, or why he's doing this. "Because…we're…we're all humans. Even though we each live different lives, we're allowed to be ourselves, who we are."

"Human?" he snaps with a deadly load of venom in his voice.

He rips another petal from the rose and I clutch the fabric covering my chest and I briefly close my eyes. The pain is getting too hard to bear.

"You're insane. People like you aren't humans. You are monsters," he roars, each word getting louder.

"Why would you say that? What did we ever do to you?" I croak in confusion.

The grudge this person holds is bigger than just the need to kill me. I have no clue why all of this hatred is aimed at me for things my kind did. And what does he even mean by my kind? Witches? My mother never mentioned anything about witches, just the rose and how it was linked to our heart…our lives.

Something crucial I now experience with each dying breath as his grip on the rose becomes more painful for me, and I feel like my insides are going to explode any second.

"Kill me," he states in an even darker tone than before.

Kill him? Who killed him? I sure didn't, I would have remembered. Besides, Hudson was very much alive when he walked out of my room a few minutes ago. He's definitely possessed by someone else, someone who was murdered. But by whom?

Another petal falls to the floor and it's as if I'm breathing through a straw that someone is teasing with by squishing it with their fingers. My heart tightens inside my chest, and there's a dull sound ringing in my ear, as if time is starting to slow. Fear grips me, knowing my life is about to end. Blood is still pouring from my eyes. It's as if someone is trying to blindfold me with a thin red veil. Everything hurts.

"What does that mean? Who killed you? Because I didn't," I yell in pain.

I need to stop him. Rip that rose from his hands. If it keeps going, there is no hope left for me, and I'll be the one he kills.

"You know this rose," he scoffs, and steps closer to me. "When the person who the rose belongs to gets killed, there's a curse that takes the life of the murderer."

He squats down right in front of me, gaze filled with utter fury. "So, you see, you people are cursed. You don't belong in this world. And since I'm already dead, I can kill you so someone else doesn't have to give up their life to end an abomination like you."

He brings the rose closer and I can tell that he's about to rip it apart with both hands.

"Wait," I yell, holding my hand up to stop him.

But the pain in my body is crippling and I need to use my arm to smack it onto the floor to balance myself.

"Your time is up. I know for a fact that you're the only one left with a rose linked to her heart. The last cursed one. It all ends here." His eyes stare into mine, a flood of hate staring at me as he rips another petal away.

Only two petals left. I curl into myself, trying to overcome the crucial pain that's crushing my bones, tightening my chest, and shredding my heart. I'm the last one? Why didn't my mother explain all these details?

We were the last two left? The one who is possessing Hudson killed my mother? He died because he crushed her rose. Which means...no. That can't be.

"Dad?" I whimper.

Please let the pain I'm enduring cause hallucinations because there's no way this is real. I'm wrong. My father killed my mother and the curse caused his death. Somehow he was able to possess Hudson so he can now kill me? His own daughter? Exactly the way he killed my mother? Oh, no. Would that mean Hudson will die too since he's using his body? Or will the possession protect Hudson because it's not really him doing the killing? Revenge. This is all about hate and revenge. How can a man kill his own wife and then come back from the dead to kill his daughter? This is some seriously twisted shit.

"Good guess." He smirks, taking a petal between his fingers.

He can't rip that one off, then there will only be one left. My life would be over. I can't let that happen. My mom gave up her life to protect me. She warned me. I failed her. I have to make this right and prove to her that we will strike back, that he can't take both our lives.

I grit my teeth and push past the pain threatening to cripple me. Shifting my body, I stare up at the man who is hiding in another body.

Keeping my voice steady I sternly tell him, "I can't let you do this."

"Why?" he mocks and plays with the petal with one finger to flip it back and forth. "It's very easy to end your life. It will only take one more second."

He slowly rises and I follow him, pushing my hands on my thighs to stay upright.

"No," I growl, wishing it was easy to fight but the truth is…I'm dying.

My body won't survive combat even if I had the skill. If I would lunge at him, he would easily rip those last two petals off and I will be dead in the blink of an eye. There has to be another way. This can't be the end.

And what if Hudson will die too? The blood of the rose is dripping through his fingers. It's his body doing the killing. The curse will take him too. Facing decades of torment all because of my father's need for vengeance. Another endless circle. No. I have to do something, anything…but…what?

A memory of earlier tonight hits me. Hudson's sweet words, his smile, his tenderness. The way he chased me down to make sure I was okay. He's a good guy. He doesn't deserve this. Maybe…just maybe… he's still in there, even if my father's spirit has taken over his body. If so, it could be our only option to save the both of us.

I take a step closer and murmur, "Hudson. I know you're in there still. I need you. Please."

Reaching out, I place my palm on his shoulder, connecting with his bare skin on mine to make a connection. To feel the way our chemistry hits when we touch.

"He isn't in control, it's not going to work, Artsy. Get that out of your head right now. There might have been a time that I actually did love you. That was before I found out about your mother and the rose. I simply can't accept what you are now, the way I couldn't accept that your mother's heart functioned on something that wasn't inside her chest. I have to do what is right for the world. And that means I have to get rid of every petal of this rose," he explains with a grin as if he's trying to distract me.

It might be working, but not for him.

All of a sudden, my mother pops up in the mirror behind him and I hear her voice flow through my mind, "You know how to get him back, Artsy. Think! You know it deep inside of your heart. I know you do."

I shake my head, trying to figure out a solution for this clusterfuck. There must be some way, somehow to come out of this alive. If only it could be as simple as to banish my dad out of Hudson so he's in charge of his own mind and body again.

Then it hits me. I know how to get him back and it's all thanks to my mother. I give her a smile and turn my head to face my dad again. I place my hand over the one that's tightly gripping my rose.

Staring deep into his eyes I soften my voice and say, "Hudson, I know you're still in there and can hear me. I don't care what you said to your friends. You turned my entire life around due to the song you wrote and the speech you gave before it. I never knew the real you before today. I'm happy to meet the side of you that is the true Hudson. That's why I'm accepting your apology. Hudson, I forgive you."

Emotions are overflowing with the pain I feel inside me. Tears are mixing with the blood and I can feel the energy slipping away from me with each beat of my heart. I suddenly realize this is it. All or nothing. If this doesn't work then he will rip off the last two petals and with it my existence.

He would have his revenge…he would have killed me the way he killed my mother. Please let it work, it just has to.

He closes his eyes and his head slowly starts to shake. I stumble back, dread filling my veins. His head shakes harder and I can feel my eyes widen at the unnatural sight before me, but it stops just as fast and then he's blinking, his gaze locking on mine.

The rose falls from his hand and slowly falls to the floor. There's only one petal attached and I know this is not a victory. No. My life will be over soon because that last petal won't take long until it falls off. It's inevitable since it's barely hanging on. I release a deep sigh. At least for now I'm still alive. All thanks to my mother who pulled me through, told me to think and act when it was needed.

"Artsy?" His voice is back to the same sweet, raspy voice I'm used to.

"Hudson," I croak, feeling dead tired, but there's a smile on my face as I try to be happy within this moment.

Though, as soon as I try to take one step forward, my knees buckle, my eyes close, and it's as if I'm stepping into an all-consuming darkness.

"Artsy. Artsy, wake up, please," a desperate voice pleads and I feel someone shake my shoulder.

"Huh?" I groan, and blink slowly.

My eyes feel dry and there's a stabbing pain in the back of my head. I rub my eyes and then scan the room I'm in. It's dark, but I recognize my bedroom. I'm lying on my own bed. How did I even end up here?

"I brought you here. You passed out. What happened? I can't remember the past hour or so. One second I walked into the bathroom, the next I was standing in the attic and barely managed to catch and prevent you from hitting the floor," Hudson says from beside me.

He looks completely drained. His hair is a mess and there are traces of dried blood on his hands and clothes.

"It's a long story," I whisper, and try to sit up.

I'm prevented from doing so when pain shoots through my limbs. Ouch.

"You need to explain what happened," Hudson demands in a firm tone and the way he's tightly gripping my hand is a little concerning.

"Okay, fine. I will explain everything soon enough, just give me time to catch my breath and gain some strength. I feel awful." I release a deep sigh and my eyes droop as I let my head fall back on the pillow.

I can't deal with the pain still throbbing through every part of my body. I should drag my tired and battered body up to the attic to make sure the rose is safely put away, but I simply can't move. Let alone focus on telling Hudson the details of my history, and to somehow make him understand what happened in the attic.

It's a hard pass. He must think I'm insane, and explaining these things to him would really shake his world on its foundation. I could really use a huge cup of coffee along with some painkillers right now, just to be able to talk about the insanity that's my life.

"Sure, I'll get you something to drink," Hudson states and gets to his feet.

He sounds somewhat annoyed, but the worry on his face shows he cares about me.

"Hudson," I croak. He stops and turns to face me when I add, "Please stay away from the attic for now. It's not safe."

He holds my stare and gives me a tight nod. I watch him leave and finally allow myself to check my body for any injuries. My knees have lacerations and when I lift my shirt I find bruises on my ribs. There's dried blood everywhere. I should check my face, but I'm guessing it's covered with dried blood as well. I should take a shower, but I don't have the energy to do so.

I can't begin to imagine what it must have been like for Hudson to be thrown into the situation. Becoming aware of being somewhere else, catching my bloody and battered body. Not knowing how he got there or what had happened. I hope I didn't traumatize him. But to be honest? Who wouldn't be after experiencing all of that? Shit. He doesn't even know what happened.

I close my eyes once more to get some rest. Completely drained, I instantly start to drift off. The pain comes back and the face of Hudson wearing a mask of evil freaks me out. My heart starts to race while my chest feels as if I'm being thrown against a wall. I open my mouth to scream, though there isn't a sound.

"Hey there...I'm back," a taunting voice states when I hear the creaking sound of the door opening.

I jolt up in my bed and scoot back against the headboard. Bile rises up in my throat. That voice. No. This can't be happening.

"We're not finished yet," the dark and deep voice tells me, drawing me back into the reality that's hitting me hard.

The man's long brown hair is hanging slightly over his shoulders. Dark blue eyes that stare hard and deadly into my very soul.

"No, not again," I whimper and draw my legs up to make me as small as I can as he walks toward me.

"We still have one petal on your rose left, remember." He smirks, and gives me a wink, as if it's our little secret that he's going to kill me.

This can't be happening. How is it possible for him to be here right now when Hudson somehow pushed him out of his body when he was possessing him earlier? My father is dead. There is no way he can be back, standing right here in my room. He doesn't seem to be a spirit, I can see him clearly, as a real person.

"You're not real," I snap and jump off the bed to get away from him when he tries to touch my face.

His features change and he's suddenly staring at me with a blank look on his face. "Not real? I have to be honest, Artsy, that hurts a little."

A sob rips from me and I try to hold strong when I tell him, "I don't care about your feelings. You're dead. There is no way you are back, standing in my room. I'm having a nightmare, that's what this is."

I throw out the words not only for him, but for myself as well. This simply cannot be real.

He sighs and steps closer, causing me to retreat into a corner of my room. "There was a moment where I truly loved you and your mother."

My father reaches out to gently slide my hair behind my ear. I slap his hand away.

"You never loved us," I growl.

He is lying. I refuse to believe that there was even the tiniest moment in his life where he cared about either of us. I lived in that house, saw with my own eyes what happened, so there's no point in lying. Even now, years later, everything is still vivid in my mind.

"Yes, I did, Artsy. I didn't know who your mother was. I instantly fell in love with her the second I saw her. It wasn't real, though. It's the curse. That damn flower ruins everything. Love is fake when it involves your family," he snarls and shoves his finger against my chest. "It's a deception to lure innocent men into a trap. You're the ones who are pure evil."

I refuse to believe there's truth to his words. It's unreal. I raise my eyebrow in challenge, but I can't prevent the tear from spilling from my eyes and feel the warmth of it slide down my cheek. A turmoil of emotions is swirling inside me and if I'm being honest? Everything sounds screwed-up.

I've always hated my father since I found him standing over my mother as she was dying. I never thought I would see him again. Let alone fight him when he possessed someone. And now I'm staring in the eyes of a murderer instead of being reminded by happy childhood memories I shared with my father. No wonder everything is screwed-up because this is my freaking reality.

"No one is capable of loving you, Artsy. Your curse will destroy the person you love for loving you. Just like your mother did to me. It's all fake." He bites down on his bottom lip as he stops talking.

I have no clue why my father killed my mother. If this was indeed linked to the rose. Though, it was he who damaged the rose and took my mother's life. No one told him to do it; it was all him. They did fight, but some of the time they seemed happy. Was their love real?

A big smile slides across his face. "I noticed you already found your victim, didn't you?"

He turns his head and I follow his gaze. Hudson steps into the room with a cup of tea in his hands.

My father turns his attention back to me. "I told you, you are just like your mother. Your destiny is to die. And I will help you get there. There will be a next time to end your life without getting interrupted. I promise. I told you honey, I am here for you."

He lets his finger glide over my cheek, a cruel smile on his face. A chill runs up and down my spine and makes my eyes flash open. I whip my head around to take in my surroundings. I'm lying in bed, covered in cold sweat, and my hair is messy and sticking to my forehead.

"Are you okay?" Hudson draws me into his arms and tells me with a soothing voice, "Looked like you were having a bad dream. You're okay now."

His eyes are wary. It must be hard and confusing for him. He doesn't remember anything from before, and now I'm freaking out again. He seems so nice and caring. Maybe... No. I won't believe anything my dad told me. I refuse to believe Hudson's feelings are not real and that he's only acting this way with me due to the curse of the rose.

My heart is still racing inside my chest. It could have just been a nightmare. My father can't be here; he's dead. It was all a nightmare. Though...it felt so real. The words he said, the way he touched my cheek, the reminders of him and my mother.

His words flow through my mind again, reminding me how everything was a deception. Hudson will end up just like my dad; that's what he was implicating. I'm not capable of love like any other person. He only fell for me because of the rose. I will destroy him all thanks to the curse.

The pain I felt from my father crushing the rose is nothing compared to what slides through me at the realization that Hudson doesn't belong to me.

"Get away from me," I snap and push his arms away so I can roll off the other side of the bed.

The tea almost spills when the cup dances on the bedside table from the sudden movement. Hudson needs to leave. I can't tell him what happened in the attic or what's happening right now for that matter. He doesn't deserve to be pulled into this mess.

"What? No, it's just me, Artsy. It was just a nightmare. You're fine now," he murmurs, not understanding the reasons why I'm upset.

"Yes, I'm perfectly fine and that's why you need to leave, Hudson," I sternly tell him.

Panic hits me at the thought of everything that could go wrong between us. My mind is racing as is my heart. He needs to leave. It's not a good time for Hudson to be around me. It doesn't matter how harsh the reality is, he just has to leave.

"Did I do something wrong?" he asks, confusion written on his face.

His voice is calm and there's sadness wrapped in his words. Dammit. I hate doing this to him, but I don't see any other way to keep him safe. I slowly shake my head, unable to answer his question with words.

"You can't simply send me away after everything that happened between us. Hell, I can't even remember what happened earlier. You still owe me a story," he snaps, somewhat frustrated.

I take a deep breath in an effort to calm down. I really don't want to do this, but I have no choice. Hudson doesn't deserve to end up like my father. I have no clue if he was telling the truth, but if he was? There's no way I could put Hudson through that.

"Leave," I growl and point at the door.

"I can't believe that I thought we were friends…more than friends. I guess you never saw me the way I saw you," he snarls in anger as he jolts to his feet.

His words cut deep and I can feel fresh tears well in my eyes.

"Goodbye, Hudson," I whisper and squeeze my eyes shut.

I can't look at him any longer; it's too painful. I don't want to hurt him, but it hurts me as well because I was so close to being happy. The crush I had on him for the longest time was finally out in the open with the possibility to finally be with him. We moved past the issues we had. He stood up to me in front of his friends…I guess I don't deserve to be happy.

"I knew my apology meant nothing to you." I hear him whisper and release a deep sigh as his footsteps slowly fade.

"I'm so sorry," I cry and try to keep myself together as I wrap my arms around me, trying to comfort myself.

Because that's all I have. Myself. I hear the front door fall shut and it feels as if loneliness just entered my body along with it. I want to run after him so badly. I yearn to be with him, to spill my guts and tell him every single detail about my history. I know I can't. I have to let him go; it's the best for the both of us.

He has a future all laid out for him with his talent and the band. He should go back to his two friends who hate me. He can be the popular guy who bullies the weird girl without worrying about my feelings.

I was never supposed to be a part of his life this way. It will only make things more complicated for him. I know I hurt him...but he will get over it. I know I won't, but this isn't about me. He should be thanking me for taking the decision away from him, even if he will never realize what it took for me to push him away. I never should have put him or myself at risk. My mother was right.

I glance down at myself, knowing all of this is my own fault. I'm covered with dried blood, my body hurting, my emotions in turmoil. A sob rips from me and I feel completely drained. As if on autopilot I move across the room to take a shower. I have to wash the evidence off my body or I'll keep falling apart. I need a fresh start and I can't do that if I'm covered with the remembrance of the past.

HUDSON

Raindrops mixed with tears run down my cheeks while I stumble through the forest. Mud covers my shoes and water soaks my clothes. Artsy allowed me to crash at her house. Then randomly her emotions took a turn and she sent me away.

I kick the dirt I pass with full-blown rage as I think about it. If I could only understand the reason why she did it. Couldn't she just see it from my point of view for one damn second? I step inside her house after giving her a huge apology. Something I never do or so much as think about.

The time after we entered her bedroom is completely erased from my memories. Then I became aware of my surroundings and barely managed to catch her, completely covered in blood. Nothing makes sense and it kinda freaks me the hell out.

I might be selfish at this point, because I feel as if I'm the only one who doesn't know what happened; only Artsy does. But she doesn't even take the time to explain it to me. I guess we're standing on opposite sides yet again.

Just like the good old days. Only this time I have an empty feeling in my chest and my gut is telling me to leave my friends. I will never go back to bullying Artsy. Everything was about to be perfect with the both of us talking things out and getting closer. Now everything is screwed-up.

The thought of her pushing me away still makes my blood boil.

Though, there's an urge deep inside me to go back and demand an explanation. Maybe she is right and we're not meant to be friends, or anything more for that matter. Dammit. Who am I fooling with my own bullshit? Of course it wasn't meant to be; we'll always be standing on opposite sides.

I keep stomping through the forest that's located behind Artsy's grandparents' house. I just want to blow off some steam. I should go home, but it's the middle of the night and it'll wake up my parents. I don't want to answer any of their questions if I don't even have answers. Besides, they think I'm spending the night at my friend's place with the concert and all.

The storm gets worse with each step that I take. Maybe I can find some place to take shelter for the night. Although the idea creeps me out, it's the only choice I have if I want to stay safe. My body is freezing and by the way the wet clothes are clinging to my body I'd say I'm not far from hypothermia if I don't get out of this freezing wind and rain fast.

My heart lurches when I think I hear the sound of branches breaking, as if someone is following me. Weird for such an abandoned piece of the forest, not to mention the crazy weather. I check my surroundings and take a deep breath to calm myself. There are no other sounds except for the wind tearing through the forest.

My foot freezes in place when I notice a tiny wooden cabin ahead of me. It looks abandoned, but that doesn't mean anything. Would it be smart to take a look? Who knows, people might still be living in there. The storm is getting really bad, leaving me no other choice but to check it out. I jump into a run and keep my fingers crossed that the cabin is indeed abandoned.

When I walk up to the door I give it a firm knock. The door moves as my knuckles collide with the wood. It makes a screeching sound, making my jaw clench because the whole evening seems like something from a horror movie. This is such a bad idea. There could be a killer living here. I'm risking my life for a place to sleep because Artsy sent me away.

I mentally groan at my rambling thoughts. Sticking to the horror movie thoughts, I might as well call out.

"Anyone here?" Yeah, I could facepalm myself for this 'cause it's the stupidest plan ever.

I wait a couple of breaths outside, but there's no answer. Great. This either means there is no one in the house, or they are wanting me to believe there is no one so they can lock me in. My overthinking, horror movie scenario, takes over. I need to just go inside and stop thinking.

"Fine," I huff to myself and push the door further open to step inside. The floorboards squeak under my feet. It must be as old as it looks. I slightly relax as I take in the rest of the cabin. It's small, but perfect for some shelter tonight. There's a bed across the room with a nightstand on each side. A closet on my left and a desk with a chair on the right. Nothing else besides old food cans on the kitchen counter and some smashed plates on the floor beneath it.

I kick the door shut and let my bag slide off my shoulder to let it land on the floor as I stroll toward the bed. I can't wait to catch some sleep after everything that happened at Artsy's place. Even though I still can't remember half of what I went through, I'm completely drained.

I glance at the bed and find a sheet that looks fairly clean that I can pull over it. I let myself fall onto it and slightly adjust the pillow under the sheet. It isn't the best bed, but at least I have a roof over my head, am out of the cold, and can get some sleep.

At least, if I would close my eyes. Though, I'm prevented from doing so when I notice the mirror hanging above the door. All I can do is stare at it. Every time I feel my eyes droop, I get a jolt through my veins, as if something is holding me back from catching some sleep. It's a weird feeling and I can't explain it.

"This is not working," I grumble and plow a hand through my hair in frustration.

Why can't I just sleep? I'm completely drained and need at least a few hours of solid sleep so I can function normally when I have school tomorrow. I have a test that's important. One I can't fail. Not to mention the fact that I still need to speak to Artsy. She owes me a huge damn explanation for throwing me out of her place.

I throw my legs off the bed to get to my feet to check out the mirror that's driving me nuts. At this point it feels as if I have no control over myself, like I am being pulled from the other side of the room toward the mirror. Before I realize it, I am standing right in front of it and staring at my own reflection.

"What the hell is going on?" I mutter to myself.

The sound of the storm raging outside doesn't have any effect on the silence in here, and all I hear is my own breathing.

"Step back," a harsh voice whispers right beside my ear.

I flinch back and whip my head around. What the hell was that?

"What do you want?" I yell and clench my hands into fists, ready to lash out at anyone who might enter the cabin.

"Look up," the same voice urges.

I can feel the warmth of its breath fanning over the skin of my neck. No, I won't look up, and I for damn sure won't look behind me.

"Are you deaf? Look up," a voice screams in my right ear.

A warm grip on my chin forces my head to tip back and stare at the mirror. Who the hell is doing this? I'm here by myself yet it feels as if someone just gripped me to face the mirror by force.

"There we go," the voice states as I glance at the mirror.

I can see the messy bed behind me along with myself standing in front of it. But there is something else behind me, more like, someone who wasn't there when I entered the room. A woman. I can't see her all that clear, though I'm sure she's there…like a shadow or something.

"Who are you? And what do you want? Are you going to hurt me?" The questions rip from me.

I need answers. There's so much strange stuff going on today. It all started this morning when I went in search for Artsy.

"Quit popping out questions. No, I am not going to hurt you. I am here to help my daughter," the woman says and is now staring right at me through the mirror, as if we're standing on opposite sides of a window.

"Who is your daughter?" I whisper with a shaky voice as I try to calm down my breathing and racing heart.

This shit is too damn weird and any sane person, including me for that matter, would have made a run for it. But it feels as if everything inside of me is screaming at me to hear her out. It's a gut thing. Like I'm supposed to stay and let her explain what's going on.

"You know my daughter. That's why I'm here, young man. I need your help, and you also need my help. So listen to what I have to say, and don't try to interrupt me. You're in danger, do you understand?" she tells me in a harsh voice to make sure I get every single word she says to me.

The last sentence makes a chill run up and down my spine. I have to stay calm. I can't interrupt her. I need to know why I am in danger and why her daughter is a part of this, even though I have no idea who that would be.

"Yes ma'am," I murmur and give her a quick nod along with it.

"Great. Sit down." She points at the bed behind me. "Don't look away from the mirror," she orders when I'm about to turn my head to follow her instruction.

I nod once more and slowly back away until the back of my legs hit the bed. I plunk down on the mattress and keep my spine straight.

"This is a very long story. I bet you're itching to find out what happened at Artsy's tonight, don't you?" she states when her reflection is right behind me in the mirror.

"Wait, Artsy is your daughter?" My eyes go wide from shock and realization.

If this is true, then this is a very important talk, and my chance to finally get some answers.

"What did I tell you? No interruptions. And yes, I am her mother. Everything will make sense when I'm done talking so just listen," she snaps, reminding me to stay quiet and let her talk.

I slowly nod while I still try to figure out inside my head what the hell is happening. I'm pretty sure Artsy's mother died years ago. There is no sane explanation as to why or how she's here talking to me. On the other hand, there's also no sane explanation as to what happened in Artsy's attic. This is why I keep my mouth shut, my eyes locked on the mirror, and my ass on the bed to hear what she has to say.

"You might have noticed that there are some things out of the ordinary when it comes to Artsy. That might also be the reason why you bullied her before you finally stepped up," she continues.

I raise my eyebrow in confusion when she mentions the bullying part. How can this woman even be aware of that little fact? It happened after she died. That right there raises a new flow of questions.

"She tells me a lot about you," Artsy's mother says, probably noticing my confusion.

"Anyway, she is very vulnerable. I never wanted this life for her. Especially not the havoc that landed in her lap this early in life. She has so many things to live for before worrying about protecting herself from her own father who wants to kill her."

My eyes go wide once more while my chest tightens. I have no idea what went terribly wrong in this family, but there has to be a load of pain and trauma by the sound of it. Though, I have no clue why she's telling me all of this or how I fit into this story.

"I can't tell you all the details because if I do, I will expose our family secret that can cost Artsy's life as well. I need you to prove to me I can trust you first. Are you still interested in hearing the rest of the story?" she questions.

"Yes, of course," I quickly state and add a greedy nod.

I hope she will trust me with the details because I simply have to know. I hated the fact that Artsy shut down and threw me out of the house. Somehow all of this is tied to what happened and the connection between us. I now realize that there's no way I can let this go.

"Thank you. Tomorrow you will go to school. I'll make sure Artsy will be there as well. Make things right between you two again. She has to be able to trust you to trust herself. At this point she feels awful and thinks she is not capable of love. She wasn't, until she met you. Even though you made her life a living hell, you've managed to touch her heart. She can't stop thinking about you and has had a crush on you since the day she saw you. By the look of concern on your face after I mentioned details of Artsy and the fact that I'm her mother I'd say you have a crush on her as well. Am I right? You stood up for her and went after her when she needed it. You want to help her."

I take a second to process everything she just said and realize she's right. I noticed her too the second I laid eyes on her. She might have been weirder than other girls and it's why I couldn't help but tease her all the time. Teasing led to bullying, though at the time I didn't realize that little fact.

Though, I did step up the second it escalated. It felt wrong to see my friends lash out, damn well hurt her. The pain, the embarrassment. Then I remember the smile on her face when I gave her the VIP ticket to my concert. Our moment when I gave the speech and sang her a song. Maybe her mother is right and I am the one to save her. But how? I know nothing about anything that's happening, especially not when it comes to details about her family.

"Just do what I said. Try to get back into her house. I will help you. Now, get some sleep," Artsy's mom says.

Before I have a chance to say something I feel the same grip on my chin I had earlier. Someone is forcing me to glance away from the mirror and face the wall instead. As soon as the grip is gone, I swing my head back to face the mirror but the woman is gone.

A deep sigh rips from me. What the hell just happened? Was it even real or am I so damn tired I started to daydream or something? I let myself drop back onto the mattress and close my eyes. I instantly start to drift off and decide everything that happened tonight has to wait till tomorrow to process. For now all I can manage is sleep.

CHAPTER 10

ARTSY

I wake up and roll to my side to check the clock on my nightstand. Five in the morning. Damn, I only slept two hours. I feel terrible, my eyes are burning and my body feels as if I was run over by a truck. I release a deep sigh, knowing I can't skip school.

There is an important test today. I really should have studied some more last night instead of going to the concert. Another thing to add to the long list of things I should have done differently yesterday.

I throw my legs off the bed and get to my feet. Black spots instantly take over my vision, making me sway. The dizziness only lasts a few seconds and I reach out to place a hand on my bed to keep my balance. Great way to start my morning.

I should have been more careful. My body went through a lot last night and instead of slowly sitting up and taking a moment to wake up, I jolted out of bed. I shake my head in an effort to clear it and take a couple of deep breaths. There. I should at least be able to take a few steps without the risk of a nosedive. Strolling to my backpack, I snatch some books out and add a few others.

I head into the bathroom to freshen up and take a minute to stare into the mirror. It feels weird seeing myself. I look miserable. Thankfully I succeeded in taking a quick shower last night or it would have been much worse.

Sadly, the trauma doesn't wash off as easily as the bloodstains. I can still feel the sharp pain in my chest when I think about what happened in the attic last night. And don't get me started about the guilt I've been feeling all night long for sending Hudson away. I hope he's okay, there was a bad storm and I just shoved him away. I really wish I wasn't so harsh on him. Though, I didn't exactly have a choice in the matter. He needs to know I can't be a part of his life. There's no future for us, and I have to protect him.

I put on a new uniform and add the hoodie my grandmother washed for me. I check my look in the mirror and wince. I look like a freaking zombie with the red eyes and black smudges under my eyes. Like I said, I have an important test today. I do hope Hudson will be there. How else would I know if he's alright if he isn't at school?

"Going to school," I bellow as I stalk through the hallway, hoping my grandparents heard me.

Opening the door, I breathe in the fresh air and relish in the cold. It's snowing and I take a step back into the house to snatch my beanie from the coatrack and let the door fall shut behind me. I stroll to school, thankfully it isn't a very long walk. I'm already drained from the lack of sleep and my body is still hurting.

A few minutes later I'm staring at the tree where I normally enjoy my peace and quiet time near school. Now it's covered with snow, but that still doesn't stop me. I throw my backpack on the ground and ease down onto it to keep my uniform from getting wet. I can't help but smile at the sight of all the snow covering the field of flowers. I love this spot.

"Hey," I whisper to no one in particular.

I take a couple of breaths, closing my eyes, letting the moment sink in for a second before I open my eyes again. I really needed that. These past few days have been crazy and completely draining all of my energy. There is way too much going on in my life, more than I can handle if I'm being honest.

I turn my face toward the foggy sky until I hear the rumble of a bike. The serenity fades when I watch how a guy rips off his beanie and reveals his messy blond hair. My eyes start to burn and I can feel my cheeks heat.

It's Hudson. The moments we shared yesterday are both good and bad. The way I yelled at him, the fear in both our eyes, the pain, the confusion. I don't think either of us realized what happened. Then I kicked him out without any explanation. There was a gap in his memory and it must have been so damn scary. Guilt weighs heavy on my heart.

Especially after the things my father said. I'm the problem here. Maybe that's the reason why I get bullied all the time. A tear rolls down

MAZE75

my cheek and I quickly wipe it away with the sleeve of my hoodie.
I shake my head to get rid of the thoughts and focus on what is
happening in front of me. Hudson is still standing beside his bike, getting
ready to walk into the building. There's a note that drops out of his leather
jacket. My curiosity is spiked and I feel the urge to rush over and pick it
up. It might be important to him, who knows.

I groan, hating myself for even thinking about helping him. I should
keep my distance for both our sake. Either way, I stand up and dash over
to the note that is laying on the snow and is slowly getting soaked.

I quickly scan my surroundings to make sure no one is watching so
I'm not caught off guard by anyone sneaking up on me. When I've made
sure there's no one in sight, I unfold the note and focus my eyes on the
words written on the paper.

"Meet me in classroom 7," I murmur the words out loud.

Was this meant for me? Or for someone else? Did he drop it for
me...or is he supposed to meet someone? That last thought makes anger
boil inside my veins. Did he forget about me this easily and is hooking
up with someone else? I read over the words once more. There is no
name written on it. The message could be for anyone.

Should I go check out the classroom like the note said? No, that
would be stalking if it's meant for Hudson. I promised myself to ignore
him and avoid any contact with him. It's for the best.

"I have to ignore it," I remind myself, annoyed by the fact that I
picked up the note in the first place.

I shove the paper into my pocket and stomp into school. I'm going
to go to class and ignore all of this, and simply pretend I never found the
damn note. As I stroll through the hallway I count up the numbers of the
classrooms I pass.

"One, two, three," I murmur, "four, five, six."

I fidget with my fingers behind my back, knowing what will come
next. I release a deep sigh and can't help myself when I come to a stop
in front of seven. I stare through the tiny window in the door. The room
seems empty and the lights are off.

Was the note a joke, or is it the wrong time or day? I shake my head.
Why did I even think it was a good idea to stop and take a look? I need
to remember what I promised to myself last night. No contact and avoid
Hudson.

I'm about to turn when the lights are suddenly on and someone is
standing in the middle of the classroom leaning against one of the tables.
A leather jacket, cargo pants, and messy blond hair. It's Hudson. He is

here, in classroom 7.

All the pros and cons slide through my head. Should I go inside or ignore Hudson and the note, and keep walking? Fuck it. I open the door and step inside the room. The sound of the door closing behind me catches Hudson's attention and makes our gaze collide.

"I erm," I start, and press my lips together. I am not prepared at all. Clearing my throat, I lamely hold up the note and mutter, "I found this."

"I knew you would pick it up." He smirks and pushes away from the table to stroll closer to me.

My heart starts to race inside of my chest. How can he affect me this much? According to my father it's the curse of the rose. I'm incapable of love and the attraction Hudson feels for me isn't real.

"What do you mean?" I raise my eyebrow in question and let my arm drop while I ball up the piece of paper.

He enters my personal space and his spicy scent enters my nose. I let my gaze wander over him to make sure he's okay due to the storm last night and me kicking him out in the middle of the night. His hair is still wet and he's wearing different clothes than last night so I guess he came home okay.

"I dropped it knowing you'd be the one who would pick it up," he proudly states.

Gritting my teeth, angry at being played like this, I whirl around and take a step forward to leave.

He places a hand on my arm and his voice is soft when he says, "Wait, Artsy. Please, I need to talk to you."

I try to shrug off his grip and snap, "I can't be near you, don't you understand? This thing between us? It's not real. I'm putting you at risk if you're near me, Hudson. You should just put me out of your mind or go back to the time when you carelessly bullied me. It's better for the both of us."

"Just hear me out, okay?" he snaps and blocks my attempt to escape.

He sounds so sure of himself. Why can't he get it through his thick skull that I'm the one who is putting him in danger? Doesn't he care? He just doesn't get it. Is there something I don't know about the situation we're in? Maybe I should hear him out.

"Fine," I huff. "Just make it quick, I don't have all day and we still have a test we can't be late for."

I'm already angry at myself for giving him a chance to spill his guts. I'm the one who's taking a huge risk by this decision.

"Look, I have no idea what happened at your house last night, but you seemed stressed and upset right after. Not to mention the dried blood all over you. It physically hurts me to know you're not okay, along with the fact that I can't do shit about it. Mostly because you won't let me. So, please, give me another chance to be your friend. I just want to help you," he pleads.

He still doesn't get it or have any idea what's going on. I don't need a friend or anyone else I'll be putting in danger. Especially not one who cares and worries about me, because my father won't let us be together.

A HEART DOOMED BY FATE

CHAPTER 11

HUDSON

I stare into her eyes and wait for her reply. My heart is pounding against my ribs and I feel as if everything in life hangs in the balance. I need for her to let me back into her house. There's no way I can keep the deal with her mother if she doesn't give me a second chance. I simply have to do this, for all of us.

"It's too dangerous. I can't put your life at risk only because you want to be friends with me." Another deep sigh rips from her.

She frowns and there's a haunted look in her eyes as if she's thinking things over inside her head. Maybe she's thinking up all the things she doesn't want me to know, or maybe things that would prevent me from getting close to her, who knows?

Leaning forward, I almost touch her nose with mine when I tell her, "Listen closely, Artsy. I would love to put myself in danger if it meant that you'd be mine in return. I've never experienced what I feel for you, and it's like you opened a new chapter in my life with just being here for me. So, if the consequences for us being together means I'm risking my own life, than that's a chance I'm going to take."

My voice is stern and direct. I'm baring my feelings, but I'm leaving out the underlying truth about the deal with her mother. Besides, I don't care about the deal anyway; the only thing that matters is that Arsty believes in me. I also need to figure out what happened in the time I lost last night. Though, I didn't expect it to be so hard to get to the truth.

We're caught in a staring match and neither one of us is backing off. I meant what I said and there's no way I'm going to let her go. The corner of her mouth twitches and her eyes start to sparkle.

"That was kinda sweet," she mutters and her cheeks heat from her admittance.

It seems I've won this round.

"So? Does that mean you're ready to give me another shot?" I grin and gently brush my nose against hers.

She gasps and steps back, allowing me to crowd her against the wall and lean my forearm against it to cage her in with my body.

"Maybe," she whispers in a teasing tone and stares up at me through her lashes.

Placing my lips right next to her ear I huskily tell her, "Scared you won't be able to resist me and completely fall head-over-heels in love with me?"

Her breath catches and she manages to croak, "You wish."

I smile against the skin of her neck, feeling her pulse jump under my lips as I place kisses along her neckline. The feeling of victory rushes through my veins.

Pulling back, I place my hand on the back of her neck to keep her gaze pinned with mine. "How do you feel about skipping class and spending the day together?"

She licks her bottom lip, making me groan. I want nothing more than to taste her and keep kissing her for the rest of the day.

Sadly, her words rip me from that thought when she says, "I already skipped so many. And not to mention, we have a test later today."

"So? One more time wouldn't matter. I think you deserve some fun, or at least a day without stress. Don't you think?" I reply and brush my lips against hers, unable to resist.

I know she's right. I can't afford to miss the test either, and my parents will kill me if they find out I'd skip this particular test. If they only knew I'd suggested it, they'd be pissed. I just had a huge argument with them about it.

Their argument ended with "you get one last chance so don't screw it up." Ugh. Yet, here I am, risking my future for a deal I have with this girl's mom. This better give me something good in return, otherwise it's all for nothing.

"Fine. Though, this might just be the dumbest idea ever." She snorts and playfully pushes against my chest before ducking under my arm to slip out from between me and the wall.

"Yeah, yeah. It's a shared effort, though," I joke, and follow her out of the classroom.

I'm torn between making things right between me and Artsy and taking the test. I need to keep my grades up and missing out on this one would mean I'd fuck things up for myself. Still, her mother told me to sacrifice everything for her in an effort to gain her trust, so this is what I need to do. Sucks, though. The torn feeling between right and wrong, not knowing what will be the best option for either of us.

"Where do you want to go?" She glances at me as we stroll through the snow.

"We could get some hot chocolate, go to your house?" I suggest, getting straight to the point.

"We could get some hot chocolate, but I don't know about going to my house." Her warm breath is visible in the cold air surrounding us.

Shit. She still doesn't trust me enough to take me home. Figures.

I jab my thumb over my shoulder to point at my bike. "Why don't we take my bike?"

"Sure," she murmurs and bites down on her bottom lip as she takes in my motorcycle.

I know she's seen me ride it. The spot she's always sitting at against the tree is near my parking space. Girls always dig the bike and I know deep down she does too. She doesn't move an inch, though.

"Let's go, or are you scared?" I challenge and swing my leg over the bike to straddle it.

"No," she snaps and jolts forward to get on the bike behind me.

I chuckle, but it's cut short when she slides her arms around me. Her front is pressing against my back and it's an indescribable feeling to have her this close. The roads are clear, and the ride is pretty damn nice. It's a bit chilly, but having Artsy warming my back lights up my entire body.

"I'm never doing that again in the winter," Artsy states as soon as I've parked in front of the diner.

She rubs her own arms and jumps from one foot to the other.

I smirk, knowing she'll have to get back on when we go back and tell her, "Sure, babe."

"What? Feel my hands. They are freezing off." She raises her hand and presses the back of her hand against my cheek.

"Okay, calm down, princess." I grin and bite down on my middle finger to take off my gloves.

Handing them to her I tell her, "Here, take my gloves."

They are way too big for her, but at least they will warm up her hands.

"Sweet," she murmurs and greedily takes them to shove her tiny hands inside.

I adore her smile as she focusses on moving her fingers in the oversized glove. She's so damn gorgeous and completely unaware of how much she affects me.

I clear my throat and ask, "Ready?"

"Heck yes. I can almost taste chocolate. That's how much I'm craving it." She giggles and jogs toward the diner.

I chuckle at her enthusiasm. This girl lightens up my day. I can't lie to myself that I'm doing it for her mother or for whatever other reason. She's everything I need in my life. I always felt like something crucial was missing, always searching for the next song or whatever the restlessness inside me craved. Now I know what was missing. Artsy.

"You coming?" she yells from the doorway, waving at me to get me to hurry up.

I shoot her a grin and run toward her to join her inside. The bell above the door jingles and the waitress behind the counter shoots us a glance.

"Hey there." The waitress shoots us a warm smile. "What can I do for you two?"

"Two hot cocoas with whipped cream, please," I order.

"I'll go find a seat while you wait," Artsy whispers in my ear and dances away to find a table.

Turning my attention back to the waitress I ask, "Can you add a slice of chocolate cake?"

"Sure." She rings up our order and I hand her the money.

The woman gets busy making our hot cocoa and I turn to face Artsy. She's sitting in a booth while happily tapping the screen of her phone.

"Here you go. Enjoy," the waitress says as she hands me a plate with the cake on it.

"Thanks, have a nice day," I murmur and wander over to the booth Artsy is sitting in.

"A hot cocoa for my girl, and something to go with it." I wait for her gaze to hit mine to shoot her a wink and place the hot cocoa and the slice of cake in front of her.

Glancing down she takes in the chocolate cake and then her eyes meet mine. "Aw, that's for me?"

I don't need any hot cocoa to warm me up, because Artsy is wearing a killer smile that warms my chest.

"Yeah, I thought you might like something sweet." I grin and slide into the booth across from her.

"I appreciate it," she shyly murmurs and her cheeks turn a nice shade of pink as she slides some of her hair behind her ear.

A tingly feeling flutters in my stomach as I watch her scoop a huge amount of the whipped cream off the drink. She tries to put all of it in her mouth at once with the golden spoon they serve with it.

"You're making a mess." I chuckle and watch how she struggles to clear some of the whipped cream from the side of her mouth.

I shake my head, knowing she's oblivious to the tiny dot near her bottom lip.

"Shame on you for not helping a girl out." She gives me a fake glare and tries to clean her mouth, and still manages to miss the spot.

I smirk and tell her, "Fine, let me be a gentleman instead of a rockstar for a change."

I reach over and place my hand on the side of her face.

"Stay still," I murmur and slowly drag my thumb over her bottom lip to catch the tiny bit of whipped cream.

Our eyes are locked and I'm completely drawn to her warm and gentle look. She's such a kind and gorgeous girl. The feelings she ignites inside me are hard to resist. All I want to do is scoop her into my arms, kiss her, and keep her safe.

"Are you still going to help me? Or are you going to try and stare it off my lip?" She tries to joke, but I hear the vibration in her voice and see the heat in her eyes; she's just as affected as I am.

I trace her bottom lip once more and pull my hand back to suck the remainder of the whipped cream off my thumb while I hold her gaze. She swallows hard while her breathing picks up. Yeah, she feels what I'm feeling all right.

"There you go." I smirk.

"Thanks," she mumbles and drags her gaze from mine.

"What? Not impressed?"

She purses her lips and says with a teasing voice, "Not really."

I jerk my chin in the direction of her plate. "Go eat your cake before I do it."

To give my words some strength I reach over to grab the plate. Her eyes widen and she smacks my hand away.

"Oh, no you don't," she snaps.

I growl low in my throat. "Now you're definitely not getting any cake."

Her eyes widen and I manage to slide the plate closer to me.

"That is cheating." She rolls her eyes. "You can't give me cake and then take it away."

"Say you're sorry for hitting me." I narrow my eyes.

"Lame," she huffs and crosses her arms in front of her chest. "I barely touched you. Besides, I'm not sorry for protecting what I considered mine. I should have hit you harder for trying to steal my cake."

I can tell she's fighting a smile, and I'm definitely fighting mine. I love how we can bounce stuff back and forth like this. Even if it's a nonsense argument.

"Apology accepted." I nod, and slide the plate back across the table.

She grips the plate and takes the cake in hand while she glares and gets ready to take a bite.

Before she does she mutters, "I didn't apologize, you weirdo."

I snort and we both chuckle. See? You just need to mess around with her a bit and she will feel comfortable enough around me again. I bet she'll suggest to go to her house soon enough. Everything is going as planned.

We chat a bit more about school and our hobbies as we finish our drinks. Time passes and with more snow coming it's getting quite dark out.

"We should probably head home. It's getting late and I don't want us to get caught in a snowstorm," I tell her and place my mug back on the table in front of me.

"Too bad, I was having fun." She sighs wistfully and checks the time on her phone.

"Well, I don't think my parents will appreciate it if I get stuck or ride in bad weather," I grumble and stare out the window, grinning on the inside that the weather is actually working with me to coax her into letting me stay at her place.

"Okay. Then you should drive us to my house, and you can stay the night so you won't have to worry about getting stuck in the snow if you have to ride across town to get to your place," she suggests with a tone that makes it seem as if she's unsure of her own suggestion. My plan falls perfectly together. I knew I could push her into a corner to leave only this as an option.

I try to act indifferent when I casually tell her, "Sure, sounds good to me."

"I'm gonna go to the bathroom real quick and then we can leave," she states and gives me one more smile as she gets up.

I nod and lean back in the booth, feeling pretty damn good about myself. I can't wait to get to her place and find out what happened last night. I also need to talk to her mother as soon as I can. I bet it won't be that easy, but it has to happen.

I figure I'll just find a mirror and try to catch her in the reflection the way she reached out the last time. I don't care what I need to do to make it happen. I won't let this opportunity slide because there might not be a next time for Artsy to invite me into her house.

A HEART DOOMED BY FATE

CHAPTER 12

ARTSY

I stroll back to the table where Hudson is sitting and point at the window. "We should go before you can't ride your bike. I overheard the waitress tell the others that they are going to close early due to the bad weather."

"Sounds good to me," he grunts and shoves his phone into his pocket as he gets to his feet.

I can't believe I'm going to let him in again. Not just as a friend, but also taking him into the house. The whole decision about keeping my distance from Hudson was blown to smithereens the moment he opened his mouth and started talking. I can't resist the guy; he's my weakness.

Deep down I know this is a bad idea, but having a friend to share things with is such a relief instead of spending my time alone. Besides, I just have to keep an eye on Hudson and not leave him running around alone in the house.

I shiver the second we step outside. The snow is falling and a gush of wind hits me right in the face.

"Cold?" Hudson chuckles.

"Freezing." I grin and we rush in the direction of his bike.

He takes a helmet out of his saddlebag and hands it to me.

"Let's race to your house." He shoots me a wink as he straddles the bike.

I give him a horrified look with the snow whirling around us. "No racing, we don't want to crash."

I'd rather go at crawl-speed instead of sliding across the road in this weather.

"It'll be fine, just hold on tight," he says with a load of confidence in his voice. He glances over his shoulder as I get on behind him. "One last thing, princess."

If I lean forward I could easily kiss him.

I don't and instead ask on a hot breath, "What?"

"I need those gloves back." He shoots me a grin that makes butterflies go crazy inside my belly.

I start to pull them off and grumble, "But then my hands will be cold."

He waits for me to hand over his gloves to tell me, "You can stuff your hands under my jacket to keep them warm, okay?"

I can feel my cheeks flush. "Fine," I murmur and slide my hands over his sides to link my fingers together under his jacket, grazing his bare stomach when his shirt rides up.

He shivers and grunts, "Damn."

"What?" I innocently ask, knowing my hands are cold.

He chuckles. "You know what you did there."

He pats my thigh with his gloved hand and then adjusts his jacket to make sure my hands are warm and cozy. I tighten my embrace and place my head against his back as he fires up the bike and heads in the direction of my house. It's dark when we arrive and there are no lights on inside.

"I hope you have keys because it doesn't look like they're home," Hudson states after he's parked the bike.

Swallowing hard, I realize, "No, I forgot. They must have gone to bed early, and I really don't want to wake them."

His eyes widen and he slowly shakes his head. "Please tell me you're joking."

I wince and huff out a frustrated breath before I tell him, "There's a secret way to get in and out of the house. My mom taught me in case something happened and I was locked out."

"Thank fuck," he murmurs. "Let's get inside before we turn into popsicles."

"One thing." I rub my hands together to get them warm while I give him a teasing smirk.

"Now what?" The corner of his mouth twitches.

I wiggle my fingers. "I'm gonna need your gloves."

"Yeah, right." He rolls his eyes, but hands me his leather gloves anyway.

A few breaths later I have them wrapped nice and warm around my hands. I stalk around the house and try to remember the instructions my mother gave me years ago. I haven't used this entrance in a while. The last time was probably when I snuck out of the house at night after my mom passed, and I needed to be alone and outside to be able to breathe.

Jumping over the fence, we get inside the backyard and stay close to the house. Shoving away the snow I search for the handle of the latch and open it. It's a small entrance and once inside there's space with only a ladder going up to the attic. I'd rather not take Hudson up there, but what other choice do I have?

He follows me up and I turn to face him and say, "Weird secret passage, isn't it?"

"Weird, but I'm happy it was there so we're inside," he states and glances back at the ladder.

"Come on." I open the door to the attic and close the small latch to cover up the secret entrance.

I speedwalk through the attic to get to the other side and get out of there as fast as possible. I do not want him up here, especially not with what happened the last time we were up here, even if my father possessed him at the time. Who knows, he might start to remember things if we stay here too long.

He follows me down the stairs and into my room.

"Finally, we made it," Hudson grunts and lets himself drop onto my bed.

I frown and can't help but tease him a bit. "I thought you were the sporty type and could run up and down stairs without getting out of breath."

He props himself onto his elbows and shoots me a wink. "That is what I want you to think."

"Lame." I snort and place his gloves onto the bedside table. "What do you want to do?"

"I don't know. Do you want to watch a movie?" he suggests and reaches for the remote on the bed beside him.

"Sounds good. You can pick one," I tell him and kick off my shoes before I jump onto the bed beside him.

"Great." A huge smirk appears on his face, and I've grown to like that look.

Though, right now it's a bit concerning and it's why I ask, "Oh, no. What are you going to put on? Horror? Action? A sappy romance?"

He snorts and starts to glance through the options. "Let me look,

I promise you it will be a good one."

Yeah, right. It does make me slightly nervous to let him pick a movie. I never have anyone over, nor do I have any friends so it's always me who picks what I want to watch.

"My personal favorite," he states and throws the remote in between us as he places his arms behind his head to settle in.

"The Conjuring," I read out loud.

"Uh huh, and we're gonna start with movie number one," Hudson tells me.

I glare at him with wide eyes. "A horror movie? Really?"

He tilts his head toward me. "What? Horrors are fun."

Yeah, right.

"Not for me," I whisper and am not looking forward to watching this movie.

I've seen some glimpses of it and the movie never appealed to me. I have too much weirdness going on in my life to add a movie to it that will definitely freak me out.

"Do you have any popcorn or something?" he asks and hits pause on the movie.

"We might have some downstairs," I reply. "Do you want me to make some for you?"

Stupid question because he wouldn't be asking, so I know I will have to go downstairs to make him some.

"If it's not too much trouble." His voice is all husky and I swallow hard at the dryness in my throat.

"Fine, but don't wander off. Stay right here until I'm back," I tell him in a no-nonsense voice as I slide off the bed.

Walking to the door, I shoot him another stern look over my shoulder and snap, "I mean it, don't move."

"Yeah, yeah, boss." He rolls his eyes.

I nod, more to myself than to him, and let the door fall shut behind me as I head downstairs. The kitchen is dark until I hit the lights and I make fast work of making the popcorn. I'm so not looking forward to watching a horror movie.

Why did I let him pick the movie? Stupid, stupid, stupid. Just as stupid as bringing him home. Releasing a deep sigh, I take the bowl of popcorn, grab two bottles of water, and silently go back upstairs. Hudson is still lying in the same spot and is gripping the remote, eager to start the movie. He looks very comfortable with his shoes off, a soft blanket thrown over him, and my fluffy pillow at his back.

"Got it," I quip and hold up the bowl.

"Sweet. Can you hit the lights?" He points at the lamp with the remote and I flip the switch to plunge the room into darkness.

"Ugh, this is way too creepy," I grumble.

Hudson chuckles. "Come on, it'll be more fun this way."

"Yeah, right. Just don't judge or laugh when I close my eyes." I release a deep sigh as I hand him the bowl and get on the bed.

"I wouldn't dare," he states with laughter in his voice. "Ready?"

"No," I snap, and pull at the blanket he's hogging to cover myself.

He chuckles. "Here we go," he murmurs and hits play. The remote lands in between us as well as the bowl of popcorn.

We're a half hour in and Hudson is watching the movie with a huge smile on his face. Mostly from laughing at me, I might add. I'm scared and have my knees up with my arms holding them tight so I can close my eyes and hide behind them. Shit. I don't think I can go across the hallway to pee, or any dark space for that matter.

Time passes and finally the movie comes to an end. The popcorn is all gone and the water bottles I brought are empty.

"And?" Hudson turns to face me. "What did you think?"

If I'm being honest, "I liked it. Though, I don't think I'll be able to be in a dark room ever again," I add as a joke.

"Glad you gave it a shot." He grins and jumps off the bed to hit the lights. "And for tonight I'm still here if you get scared."

My heart melts as I think about what he said. He offered to protect me and it's something that's been lacking in my life.

"I'm gonna head into the bathroom to freshen up and get ready for bed. Sound good?" he asks and throws a thumb over his shoulder.

I'd rather not have him walking out on his own, not just due to the scary movie, but more about what happened the last time. On the other hand, I can hardly refuse the guy to head into the bathroom.

Unease fills my veins and it's why I grumble, "Are you really going to leave me alone after the movie we just watched?"

He doesn't so much as blink when he offers, "You can always join me if you like."

My heart skips a beat and I can feel my cheeks heat. "No, thank you."

He gives me a wolfish grin. "I'll be right back. Yell if you get scared."

I flip him off and he chuckles. Should I check the hallway to make sure he's in the bathroom and is not wandering off to the attic? Minutes pass. Adrenaline spikes and I end up tiptoeing to the door. The sound of footsteps jolts my heart.

"Boo," Hudson snaps as he steps inside.

I swear I almost jump out of my skin and scream like the girl I am. Hudson bends over with a deep belly laugh. Stalking to the bed, I grip a pillow and smack him against the head.

"Asshole," I snarl.

"Calm down, princess. We don't want your grandparents waking up." He chuckles and rips the pillow from my hands to throw it on the bed.

"Are you tired?" he rumbles and steps closer.

"Sort of," I breathe and back up in the direction of the bed.

He reaches out and gently cups the back of my neck to pull me close. His mouth covers mine and the kiss that follows drives away all the dark thoughts of the movie. Warmth spreads through my veins and a tingling feeling ignites in my lower belly.

I can feel how hard he is when he presses against my belly. I want him and I groan into his mouth to let him know how much he affects me. My hands roam over his chest and I start to tug at the material.

I want to feel my hands on his skin and explore every inch of his body. Somehow I land backwards on the bed. A giggle rips from me and it's cut short when I watch Hudson grab the back of his shirt to pull it over his head.

His lean chest is exposed for my eyes only. I felt the hint of a six-pack when I straddled his bike and wrapped my arms around him earlier today, but seeing it? Wow. My breath catches when his hands move toward his belt.

I start to peel away my own clothes to settle under the blankets. There's no time to feel self-conscious, and even if there was, the heat in Hudson's gaze would let me know that he wants me and more than likes what he sees.

He holds up something he pulled out of his wallet and I nod. His gaze stays locked on mine as he slides into bed next to me. I'm highly aware of my own body and I long for his touch and closeness. Just as much as I want to touch him, feel how hard he is for me in the palm of my hand.

The gentle way he cups my head and kisses me is completely enthralling. I feel special, adored, and completely safe with him as he covers my body with his. I gasp when I feel him between my legs and dig my nails into his back when he slowly enters me.

He stares into my eyes. It's intimate and there's nothing else in this world except us and the way our bodies connect. He starts to slowly move inside me, both of us groaning and gasping at the intense feeling our bodies create.

His lips find mine and our kiss becomes a way to communicate. Every emotion I feel I pour into the kiss and I receive the same in return. The moment is perfect and soon enough we share a pleasurable intimacy that makes my heart race.

It's a building pleasure that needs to explode. I don't ever want it to end and yet I want to experience the earth-shattering bliss I know is coming. He buries himself deeper inside me with each stroke and I urge him on.

My nails dig into his back and I cling to him. The overwhelming bliss hits me out of nowhere and I moan his name. His movements become erratic and then he's exploding inside me. His lips are near my ear and he spills my name in adoration on a hot breath. Completely out of breath we cling to one another and our legs stay tangled.

He nuzzles my neck and murmurs in a raspy voice, "You're perfect, Artsy."

I close my eyes and let our special moment sink in along with his words. I let my fingers slide through his hair when I murmur in return, "It's you who makes me feel perfect."

We fall silent, but after a moment Hudson gets up to go to the bathroom. When he returns I quickly freshen up as well. We both end up in bed again, wrapped in one another's arms. I never thought this would happen. Let alone find out that Hudson likes to cuddle. Minutes pass and worries settle in.

"Hudson?" I whisper, hoping he's still awake.

"Yeah?" he mumbles, but keeps his eyes shut.

"Please don't wander around. And if you do need to leave the room? Please wake me up first, okay?" I ask, hoping he'll listen and won't wander off.

Maybe I should stay awake and make sure? Except, I'm sleepy so I'm pretty sure I won't be able to stay awake for long.

He opens one eye. "Scared of a doll, Artsy?"

The corner of his mouth twitches and I know he's teasing me about being scared due to the movie. But this isn't about the freaking movie; this is about my reality.

"Shut up. I mean it, Hudson. This house is scary at night," I warn in the hopes it convinces him to stay in bed, or to wake me up first.

"Whatever you want, princess. Besides, I'm right where I want to be." He sighs in contentment before snuggling even closer.

"Night, Hudson." I smile, feeling happy for once.

I adore him and he sure makes me feel adored by him. After days filled with chaos and emotions it's a relief to feel completely at ease in his strong arms. I'm glad I gave him another chance, even though I still have doubts, because my father could be right. I don't want to believe it, but what if it's true? This feels like a dream, to finally be with Hudson.

It's scary because my mother had the same strong bond with my father before it all fell apart. Will that be our destiny as well? Is my heart doomed by fate? I glance at Hudson's face who is completely at ease.

I don't want to accept it. I need him. What we just did was special and brought our connection and relationship to a whole new level. My emotions are all over the place. I don't want to lose what we have, but am I putting my heart and life on the line by being with him?

Sleep starts to claim me and I decide to trust Hudson and let go of my worries for tonight. I'm allowed to feel happy. To enjoy the safety and warmth of Hudson's embrace and feel adored by him. I snuggle closer to Hudson, who is already asleep, and allow myself to drift off as well.

CHAPTER 13

HUDSON

I blink at the darkness of the room and stretch my arms out over my head. The curtains are still closed so I have no idea if the sun is up already. The soft body of Artsy shifts against me and I smile down at her. She's amazing and sure felt perfect when I made her mine last night.

Smiling, I turn my head and glance at the clock on the bedside table. I frown when I notice it's only two-thirty in the morning. I sigh and cuddle closer against Artsy. Closing my eyes, I get ready to drift off when I hear something. It sounds like it's coming from the hallway. Was that a voice?

Shit. It must be the movie from last night messing with my head. I close my eyes again and try to get back to sleep. Except, I have a gut feeling that something bad is about to happen. Annoyed, I sit up and stare at the door as I hold my breath in an effort to keep things quiet so I might hear it better if the voice calls out again.

There's only silence and I release a deep breath. Yeah, it's definitely just me and clearly I need more sleep. I shake my head and let myself drop back down onto the bed. I snuggle closer to Artsy and cover the both of us with the blanket.

The second I close my eyes I hear the voice again. Someone is whispering and it's coming from the hallway. This time it is much clearer. My eyes fly open when I hear my name.

"Hudson," someone calls out, louder this time.

I jolt out of the bed and stare at the door. Everything inside of me is urging me to check to see what's going on. I glance at Artsy, knowing I should wake her because she asked me to. Hell, the last time crazy things happened too. I might not remember and that right there makes it crazy things.

Though, Artsy is sleeping peacefully and I hate to wake her up. Maybe it's just her mother who is trying to contact me again. Now that might have been weird as well, but it made sense somehow. Maybe I should check to see if it's her? That's safe enough, right?

I gently slide out of bed, careful not to wake Artsy, and reach for my jeans. Once I've put them on, I take my phone and shove it into my pocket. Opening the door, I take one last glance over my shoulder to make sure Artsy is still sleeping before I step out into the hallway.

"Hello?" I whisper and look left and right, finding no one there.

My heart is racing inside my chest and I release a deep breath. It was just my imagination. I definitely shouldn't have watched a horror movie before we went to sleep. That's probably why my nerves are all over the place.

Screw it, I'm going back to bed.

I'm about to turn when I hear a scratchy voice. "Attic."

The attic. The place where it all went down last time. Well, there's still a gap in my memory, and that's where I found myself with a bleeding Artsy. But if it's Artsy's mom trying to get me to go up there, I have to go. Crap. Why does it have to be the attic in the middle of the night? Everything seems off and the gut feeling that something bad is bound to happen creeps up on me once again.

Gritting my teeth, I check on Artsy one last time and walk in the direction of the stairs. It's dark and I have to use the flashlight of my phone to make sure I don't stumble and break my neck. The door to the attic is open and a chill runs up my spine due to the memory of the last time I had to carry Artsy covered in blood out of there.

This is such a bad idea. A chilly gush of air flows over my back and I shiver. Steeling myself, I step into the empty room.

"Okay, I am here. What do you want from me?" I grunt and try not to feel as freaked out as I definitely am.

"Good to see you again, Hudson," a female voice states and the lights come on.

A sigh of relief flows from me and I turn off the flashlight of my phone and tuck it into my jeans pocket. For a second there I thought I was going to face some kind of demon or a ghost or whatever.

Definitely too much movie time if you ask me. Though, some believe in it. The things I've experienced the past few days? I have to admit that I have no clue what to believe...other than knowing something more is out there.

"Are you Artsy's mom?" I ask, just to make sure.

"Good guess," she replies, and I now realize it's the exact same voice I heard back in that cabin when she showed herself in the mirror.

"Why did you want me to come up to the attic?" I tilt my head and walk further into the room, feeling a bit more confident to know that it's her.

"I promised to give you some answers if you were able to win my daughter's trust back. You clearly did since you're standing here. So, I am going to keep my promise as well," the woman explains.

Her tone of voice sounds nice and honest. Though, my gut tells me that there's something off about all of this. As if there might be consequences to the promise she's talking about.

"Alright," I carefully state, feeling unsure about the whole thing.

"Sit down," she orders.

I find myself in front of the large mirror and sit down in front of it. My reflection is staring back at me and then there's a woman coming up behind me. She looks like the one I saw in the mirror at the cabin. She takes a seat on the pillow beside me.

"Hudson. I know you will agree, because you want answers, but I have to hear you say the words. The information I'm about to give you is dangerous, do you understand?" Her tone holds warning and the stern look on her face shows she means it.

"I understand and I accept the consequences. I want to know what happened to me and what is going on with Artsy and this place," I tell her and ignore the fact that she mentioned it's dangerous.

I hate not knowing the truth, and I'm already in too deep when it comes to Artsy.

"Good. There is only one thing I didn't tell you." A grin slides across her face. "I wasn't totally honest with you the last time."

Her voice holds a mysterious tone to it and if I'm being honest? It's scaring the crap out of me.

I clench my teeth and hiss, "What do you mean?"

"I promised I'd tell you the story, but you have to do something to make that happen. Something that will change your life and will pull you into the kind of danger that can easily rip you from this world." Every word she says freaks me the hell out.

I should have stayed in bed with Artsy. Why did I check out the voice and come up here? Shit. I'm doing this for Artsy, and for myself to find out what's going on.

Releasing a frustrated breath, I grunt, "What do I need to do?"

A bone-chilling laugh flows through the air, and then she says, "Play the Ouija board."

I can feel my eyes go wide. There's no way I'm going to play or so much as touch a Ouija board. I like horror movies just like any other person, but to get involved in that? Attract demons and shit? No way.

"Still want to know the truth? Or are you too scared?" she challenges.

Where I got chills up my spine earlier, I'm sweating like a pig now. There's an internal battle going on inside me. On one hand I want to know the truth, and I have to push through whatever obstacles I might face. On the other hand? Ouija board. Not a game. Shit like that is as freaky as putting your life in the balance and seeing if you live to see another day.

"I can't," I croak and slowly shake my head.

"So, you don't want to know the full background story, and figure out what happened the last time you were up here in this attic by yourself?" she challenges.

"I was up here by myself? I was here with Artsy," I murmur and frown, wishing like hell I could remember.

"What's your answer, Hudson? Yes, or no. It's as easy as that," she snaps, completely ignoring my question.

Though, the real question is…am I ready to play with my life and find out everything I want to know? Would it be worth it? Maybe it's all in my head, a nightmare I'm gonna wake up from any second. Besides, the stuff in movies hardly ever happens in real life, right?

"What do you have to lose?" someone whispers beside my ear.

She's trying to pressure me into doing it. Risk my own life to meddle in her daughter's life. No. I can't do this. Though, somehow the word "no" isn't tumbling over my lips. Is the woman manipulating me? Or am I considering the possibility of submitting to her request?

Happy moments I shared with Artsy flow through my mind. It's as if she's giving me highlights to remind me why I need to do this.

"Yes or no?" she growls. "My patience is running thin."

I need to make a decision. The movies I've seen of people playing with a board have experienced crazy shit, but I don't think they died. Haunted? Yeah. Crazy stuff happening? Definitely. Though, if I follow the rules and play the game like it's supposed to be played…it can't hurt me. Right? Decision made.

"I'll do it," I tell her with a load of confidence. Yet, I instantly regret my answer.

"That's what I like to hear." The woman smiles with satisfaction. "The board is behind the box beside the mirror. You should hurry, someone could wake up, and the sun will rise soon."

I nod and reach for the box. There's a tension leaving my body, as if I'm no longer held hostage. A confirmation that she had some kind of hold on me, and when I shift my body there's the same pull once again. A creepy thought enters my brain that I'm only free to move when I follow her orders, and otherwise I'd be trapped in this room.

I shake off the thought and open the box. I find the Ouija board hidden inside, just like she said. What the hell am I getting myself into? A mere few days ago I was just a guy teasing a girl. A change of heart had me stepping up and in a whirlwind I find myself doing shit I'd never thought I'd experience; I'm the guy who watches creepy movies, not plays the main part in one.

"I'll give you step-by-step instructions. Although, I'm guessing you already know how to play, don't you?" Her mysterious voice flows through the air once again.

Sometimes it feels as if she can see right through me, know my every thought. Either that or she's manipulating me and pushing me into doing her bidding.

"Maybe," I grunt and scoot back to the place in front of the mirror.

From the corner of my eye I notice a delicate rose, but I don't give it a second thought because the woman is giving me more orders. "Now, you go to the other box on the left. There are four candles in there and a lighter. Grab those too."

I get to my feet and do as she says, finding four red candles and the lighter.

"Now what?" I ask when I've placed the items next to the board and glance into the mirror.

"Turn the lights off and light the candles." The voice sounds as if the woman is sitting right beside me, and yet it's also like she's inside my head.

It's unnerving to say the least. I don't exactly have a choice as I get up and hit the lights. The mirror holds a soft glow and I stalk back to the spot where I was sitting. I stare down at the Ouija board and the candles. This is a mistake. I need to turn around and get the hell out of here.

"Sit down," the woman snaps.

Without thinking I drop to my knees and grab the lighter tightly in my hand. One by one I light all the candles until all four of them are burning.

"Good. Now place the board in the center to get ready," she instructs me.

Every cell inside my body is screaming at me to stop. I shouldn't get the board ready and yet I place it on the floor in front of me with the planchette on top and in the middle of it.

"Begin." This time her voice is low and dark.

Like she is itching to become or do something evil. I don't like this idea at all. With shaky hands I place my index and middle finger on top of the planchette. A gush of freezing wind enters the room and makes me shiver.

HUDSON

I let a minute pass while my eyes glance at the clock that is hanging on the wall on my left.

"Three AM," I read the time out loud on a whisper.

"Devil hour, perfect timing don't you think?" The woman in the mirror smirks.

At this point she knows damn well what kind of danger she's putting me in. I release a sigh and mentally prepare myself for this moment. I move the planchette over the board, sliding it three times in a circle until it hits the middle again.

"Ouija board, I'm here," I whisper with a nervous tone.

My fingers are glued to the board, too scared to let go by accident. I swallow hard when I catch sight of the flame of the candles that are flickering without a gush of wind.

"If anyone is here, can you move the planchette to 'yes'?" I question, following the instructions I've seen people do in the movies.

The planchette starts to slide over the board without me pushing or guiding it. A jolt of adrenaline hits my veins and my heart begins to race. The planchette slides over the letters and numbers until it hits the "yes" and comes to a stop.

No way. No damn way did that just happen. I keep staring at the board and I know I have to keep going.

"Who are you? Can you spell your name with the letters on this board?" My hands are shaking so bad and it's hard to keep myself together.

Yet, I know I can't let go. I just can't. A couple of seconds pass, but it feels more like minutes, until the planchette starts to move by itself again. It goes in one straight line to the first letter.

"G," I read out loud through the glass, and then it shifts to the next letter. "R." It moves again. "I." I keep staring, unable to look away. "F." The planchette slightly moves and returns to the same letter. "F," I repeat. Then it moves to the next. "I." And the last one. "N." Before it stops.

"Griffin?" I blurt, quickly pasting the letters together inside my head. "Is your name Griffin?" I ask to make sure I'm right.

In the blink of an eye the planchette slides to the "yes" in the corner. That's his name. Holy shit, it's working.

"Do you know a Griffin?" I ask when I glance at the mirror.

She's still watching me and her lips turn into a straight line. "Even you know him, you saw him before."

I frown and wonder what she means by this? I don't know any Griffin.

Glancing back at the board I ask, "Do you know who I am?"

My heart lurches when my hands move automatically with the planchette as it slides to the "yes." So, this Griffin knows who I am. But how does he know me?

"Can you tell me where you know me from?" I ignore the rush of cold wind flowing over my skin.

This is as creepy as it can get, but there's no way I can stop. It's both intriguing and terrifying. My gaze stays fixed on the board as I watch the planchette move to spell out a word.

"Here," I state, connecting all the words.

Here? Does that mean this Griffin saw me in this house? Or, maybe in the attic?

"That's not possible. I've only been in this house once before and there wasn't a Griffin, and I haven't touched this board before today. It's simply not possible," I murmur to myself as I think things over.

"Like I said, you've been up here before," Artsy's mother says from beside me.

I slowly shake my head. That's not possible. Unless...I've only been up here when I caught Artsy, covered in blood. I didn't have a clue what happened. Did I meet this Griffin during the time where my mind is a blank?

I take a deep breath to steel myself. "Did you see me when I was in the attic the last time I was here?"

I'm not sure I want to know the answer, but I asked the question anyway.

"Yes," I read the word the planchette shows me.

Shit. Something bad did happen and all I have is a huge hole in my memory. Is that the reason why Artsy was acting so strange, and why she kicked me out for no reason? Did I do something? What the hell happened up here?

My mind is overflowing with different scenarios and multiple questions. I want all the answers, but I do have to ask the right questions to get them. Right now I want all the details, but on the other hand...I also don't want to hear if...if...shit, Artsy was covered in blood. That right there points to something horrific.

It happened. Artsy is safely sleeping in her bed. I'm right here and I need to know.

"What happened when I was in this attic before today?" I ask, even if I'm afraid to hear the details.

The planchette starts to move on its own again and spells out four letters.

I frown when I connect them and state, "Show."

What does Griffin mean by show? That doesn't make any sense as an answer to my question.

"What do you want to show me?" I wonder out loud, without thinking twice about what I'm asking.

I wait, but nothing happens. I shiver. Is it getting colder in here or is it me? Why isn't the planchette moving? Am I doing something wrong? There's silence and I start to freak out. The only thing I can think of is moving the planchette to "goodbye" to end it.

A sharp pain flares up in my lungs and I'm unable to catch my breath. It's as if someone just kicked my chest to shove me back...into nothing? Darkness is surrounding me. I blink a few times to adjust to the dark and faintly see the candles scattered across the floor, candlewax dripping everywhere.

I try to scream, "Stop it," but I can't even pry my lips open. There's no air in my lungs left to cry out and I'm starting to get dizzy.

The planchette jolts under my hands and slides to the "no" on the board.

No? What does it want from me? Is this Griffin's way of showing me what happened? This isn't making any sense. This is not how this game is supposed to go. Did I mess up?

The scene before me shifts. Gone is the board and the candles and instead I see a table across from me that holds a flower. A rose. Instead of darkness there's a white light surrounding it.

The pain in my chest stops and I'm finally able to take a breath, but the second I do? My heart starts to pound.

"Where am I?" I croak and hear my own voice echo around me.

"Showing you," a dark man's voice filters through the air.

Is that Griffin talking?

I'm staring at the attic from a different point of view, as if I'm not myself but looking in. I can't explain it, but it's like watching a movie play out in front of you. A very real one. My heart is racing and the pounding inside my head becomes louder. It's the same attic, but there's no sign of the Ouija board or the candles. The place I was sitting in is not where I'm standing right now.

A sound catches my attention and it's hard for me to focus on what happens next. I watch myself step into the attic. Me. How is that possible? The other me is walking to the table with the rose. It's the same one as the patch on the leather vest I had on during the concert. Black with red lines.

There's a man wearing black clothes standing beside the table. His hair is messy and in a shade of red that's definitely dyed. The man's eyes are looking straight at me, there are bruises, scars, and recent wounds all over his face. Just looking at him gives me the creeps.

He doesn't say anything, just stares with a sinister smirk on his face.

"Who are you?" I manage to push the words out of my mouth.

"Griffin," the man states.

It's the same voice as the one I heard when I was using the Ouija board. How can this be? What the hell is going on? I clearly don't remember seeing or talking to this man and yet I see myself standing near him and am witnessing it. Is this what happened during the time I lost that night?

"You must be Hudson. Good to see you. I've been trying to talk to you for years," Griffin says to the other me in the room.

The other me gasps and asks, "How do you know my name?"

"That doesn't matter, all that matters is that you're here now. And I can use you to get what I want." He grins and leans in closer to the other me.

"Don't hurt me, please. I will leave," I hear myself beg.

Pain fills my body, as if acid is burning through my veins. This doesn't feel right. This man is evil, I know it deep down and as I witness how he's confronting me? I'm more afraid than ever to find out what happened during the gap in my memory.

"I don't want you to leave," Griffin states and is gripping the other me.

"Please," I hear myself beg and start to struggle.

There's nothing I can do but watch myself and Griffin. This is what he meant by "show." I'm locked in place to see what went on the first time I was in the attic. What happened before I caught Artsy covered in blood.

"Stay still. I'm just going to use you for a little while. Artsy needs to know what she has done and what her mother did." Griffin's hands go to my head, and he places them on my temples.

I might be seeing it as a bystander, but I feel every inch of pain I'm experiencing in that moment. His fingers feel like a hot flame on my skin and are burning a hole through my skull. The pain becomes unbearable and I fall to my knees. Dark spots enter my vision and I suddenly feel completely different.

When I stare at myself across the room, I notice Griffin is gone. Though when I really look at my other self, I become aware something is very wrong. The movements I make feel unnatural, as if someone is pulling strings and I'm the marionette that's being controlled.

I watch how the other me grabs the bowl protecting the rose and lets it crash to the floor. Snatching the rose, I feel how the thorns bite into the flesh of my hands. All I can do is stare and know deep down that's not me controlling my body.

A noise draws my attention to the door. Artsy is standing there with a horrified look on her face and it's all directed at the other me. When the hand tightens on the rose I can tell it gives her pain. Horrible pain. As if crushing the rose is crushing her and there's blood leaking from her eyes. Holy shit, this is insane. She's yelling at the other me, trying to make the pain…my actions stop.

The screaming makes my head throb, my vision becomes blurry, and I feel as if I'm going to pass out. Suddenly I'm sitting down and staring at the Ouija board on the floor in front of me. No sign of the other me, or Artsy for that matter.

Holy shit. Did Griffin do this? Somehow he's thrown me back in time to witness what happened during the gap in my memory? But how? He's a ghost. Wait. Is a spirit that strong? Letting me see things from the past I completely forgot about? I direct my attention back to my fingers that are still safely on the planchette. I guess I have my next few questions for Griffin ready.

I'm about to voice my first question when I hear the sound of footsteps approaching. Someone is clearly walking up the stairs. Shit. Is it Artsy? She cannot find me here. Without thinking things through I jump up and let my fingers leave the planchette.

I whip my head in the direction of the door and start to freak out. Suddenly I remember the escape tunnel Arsty showed me; the way we slipped into the house earlier. I move silently through the room and open the latch. The footsteps sound as if someone is going to enter any second and I quickly shut the latch and descend the stairs.

Coming to a stop at the end, I open the hidden entrance and slip outside. Locking up behind me I run through the backyard, jump over the fence, and head for my bike. I have to get out of here.

CHAPTER 15

ARTSY

A chill runs up my spine when I push the door to the attic open. There's a flickering light in the darkness that catches my attention. For a fraction of a second I think it might be fire, but then I notice the candles on the floor. I huff in frustration. Who would leave candles burning on the floor?

My eyes widen when I notice the Ouija board that's surrounded by the candles. A jolt of fear runs through my body as I stare at the scene in front of me. Such a creepy thing to see after watching a horror movie. Who would do this? My grandparents wouldn't, of that I'm sure. Hell, I never knew there was a Ouija board up here. Someone must have brought it with them. But who?

Definitely something to find out, but not now. This whole thing is freaking me out and I want to leave. I wince and realize that I have to blow out the candles, can't risk burning the house down. Taking a few deep breaths in an effort to calm myself, I realize it doesn't help shit because I'm still freaked out and rooted to the ground.

"Be brave, you got this," I murmur to myself and shuffle closer to the board and the candles.

When I reach the board, I slowly squat down and blow out the candles one by one. I glance at the Ouija board and it's then I notice that someone left the planchette in the middle of the board. Oh no. Shouldn't it be on the 'goodbye' if they ended the session? I mean, that's what I've always seen them do in the movies.

'ne person who was here didn't say goodbye to the
'nere in the attic. Not that I'm an expert at these
'nat you need to say goodbye, otherwise the spirit
...nd it will follow you.

...n definitely starting to freak out. I only come up here to
...nom or to protect and check on my rose. I can't let someone
 ...y it like last time. The rose is still recovering, but it looks as if
some of the petals are already growing back. Though it will take a while
for it to be completely back to full bloom.

A rustle comes from behind the boxes all the way in the back. I can't
see because of the darkness that is surrounding me. I slowly rise and with
it I knock one of the candles beside me over. Wax spreads onto the floor.
I ignore it and let my gaze roam over the room. A chill runs up my spine,
causing the urge to run away.

The thought of what happened here with the candles and unfinished
session with the Ouija board cause me to whirl around and head for the
door. I slam it shut behind me and rush down the stairs to get to my own
room.

I jump onto the bed and scramble to get under the covers. I'm
completely out of breath and try to wrap my head around what just
happened. Something…someone is up there doing stuff, and I'm fairly
sure it's not my mother. She wouldn't do that to me. Did something
happen to her?

She's a spirit and it's possible to communicate with her through the
board. But who would do such a thing? No one's here besides me and my
grandparents. They'd never…and it's then I remember. Hudson. I invited
him to stay the night.

We entered the house through the secret passage. I never felt him
getting out of bed, or leaving for that matter. Was that him up in the
attic? Using the secret passage to slip out of the house? But why would
he do that? He didn't remember what happened up in the attic; he was
possessed by my father. Why would he go up there again? Oh no. What
if it happened again?

Maybe I'm just paranoid. Hudson could still be in the house or simply
went home without saying anything. I glance at the bedside table where
his phone was when we crawled into bed together. It's gone. Releasing
a frustrated huff, I grab my own phone and shoot off a message, asking
where he is.

At this point I don't even care if it was Hudson up there doing
whatever it is he was doing. I just need to know if he's okay. Okay, I do

have to know what kind of ritual happened up in the attic. If someone scared off my mother and I'd never see her again I'd be devastated.

I stare at my phone and wait for any kind of response from Hudson. After ten minutes there still isn't a reply and I can tell he's never read my message either. Something is definitely wrong. Drawing my knees up, I place my chin on my knees and stare at the door, too afraid to sleep.

For all I know there was someone up in the attic summoning demons or whatever.

I could wake up my grandparents, but I don't want to bother them. Especially when they probably have no idea what happened. I'd also have to explain the fact that I invited Hudson over, but then again, it might not have been him up there. Everything is so confusing and frustrating, creepy as hell on top of it.

I guess there's nothing left to do other than wait till morning to see if he shows up at school. We need to have a discussion, and if he doesn't show up? Then I have to find him, even if I have no clue where to look. Either way, I don't feel safe in this house anymore.

Though, it's not like I can't leave; I have nowhere else to go. My rose needs to stay here because my mother is up there who protects it. If she's still up there that is. No. I refuse to think otherwise.

The rest of the night I spend watching funny videos on my phone in an effort to distract myself and not freak out by every single noise I hear. It is driving me insane. Finally it's time to turn off my alarm and get out of bed to get ready for school.

I feel like dead weight on my feet. With almost no sleep, nerves shot to hell, and my mind running fifty miles an hour, I'm completely drained. My head is pounding as I stare at myself in the mirror, wincing at the way I look.

A yawn escapes me as I take in the dark smudges under my eyes. I look awful. Taking a quick shower, I get ready for school and have to add sunglasses to my outfit to hide my tired and burning eyes. I glance at my backpack and realize there's no need for me to take it with me. The reason I'm going to school is to find Hudson. There's no way I can focus on class or anything else.

I grab my phone and check my messages. He still hasn't replied or seen my message. Walking down the stairs, I sneak out the back to avoid any confrontation with my grandparents. It's still a little dark outside when I start to stalk down the street.

It doesn't take long until I arrive at school. The first thing I check is the space where Hudson always parks his bike. Disappointment hits me when I find it empty. His bike wasn't at my house either so I know he left with it, which means he's not at school either.

I do have to make sure before I waste my time looking for him elsewhere. Jogging into school, I wander through the long hallway and instantly all eyes are drawn to me. I pull my hood down and keep my glasses in place as I ignore everyone around me.

I stumble onto Hudson's friends near the lockers at the end of the hallway. I completely freeze up when the bad memories assault me. These two have hurt me the last few times I ran into them. Every cell inside my body warns me to walk away, knowing how badly they bullied me to the point of assault the last time.

Except, I need to talk to them. They might know where Hudson is.

Bracing myself, I take a deep breath and step forward. "Hey."

They don't even acknowledge me and keep talking to one another. The loud noise of the people around me might have swallowed my voice so I need to do it again.

This time I firm my voice and snap loud, "Hey."

One of them throws me a dirty look and assesses my sunglasses and hoodie. "Who are you?"

"What do you need there, girl?" the other one quips.

I swallow hard. "Did either of you see Hudson today?"

"Why do you ask?" one of them asks with a deep frown on his face.

"I have to give him something he asked me to bring, that's all." I shrug as if I don't care if he's here or not.

The guy with dark hair turns to the other. "Did you talk to him today?"

He shakes his head. "You?"

"Nah, I only saw him talking to that blonde girl, the one who walks around trying to tell everyone to wear crystals all the time," the one with the dark hair states and turns to me. "Well, there you have it. Now run along, girl."

I bob my head and slink away, thankful that they didn't recognize me with the hood on and my sunglasses. Either that or they are too busy with other things instead of being bored enough to bully others.

Anyway, I know exactly who he was talking about. The girl who is always talking about crystals is Abbi, and my mission now is to find her.

She mostly hangs out in the biology classroom, I should check there first. I've known her for quite some time. She used to be one of my friends before my mother died. Stalking in the direction of the classroom, I find it empty except for Abbi who is completely engrossed in the book that's lying on the table in front of her. That was easy to find her. Hopefully she can point me in the right direction to find Hudson just as easily.

"Hey, Abbi." I wave and stroll toward her when she raises her head.

"Hey?" she warily says and glances behind me.

She seems skittish and I give her a smile as I tug down my hood and slip off my sunglasses. "It's me, Artsy."

"Oh, hey, what's up?" She smiles.

I grab one of the chairs near her and take a seat. "I heard you saw Hudson today. Do you happen to know where he might be now? I need to give him something and I seemed to have missed him this morning."

I use the same excuse I gave his two friends, hoping she'll give me the information I need.

"Hudson, yeah…I saw him today. He needed some sage," she muses as she dives right back into the book she was reading before I stepped into the classroom.

"Did he happen to mention why he needed it?" I ask.

She shakes her head without looking at me. "No. But he was looking really bad. I gave it to him for free because it looked like he really needed it, and I felt sorry for him."

"What do you mean, he looked bad?" I wonder, a chill runs up my spine at the reminder of what I found in the attic.

"His eyes were bloodshot, as if he skipped a night of sleep or cried his eyes out before he found me. He was a complete mess with wrinkled clothes and all. He didn't say anything else except for the rambling about the sage he needed." She glances up and gives me a concerned look. "There was definitely something he was freaked out about and needed cleansing, it's why I gave him the sage for free."

"Okay. Thanks, Abbi, I really appreciate it," I tell her and get to my feet.

"Wait. You said you needed to give him something, right?" she asks and I turn to face her once more.

I bob my head. "Yeah."

"I don't know if it'll help, but I heard him mumble to himself when he walked away. He said something about going to a place in the forest to hide and stay away from people," Abbi explains.

"Thanks, it helps," I assure her and give her a thankful look.

I rush out of the classroom and jog down the empty hallway. I have to go home and grab a few things before I go out to search for Hudson. If Abbi is right about the way Hudson looks, and needed the sage, then it's even worse than I thought. Something bad definitely happened in the attic last night and I have to help him, even if it was wrong of him to go up there in the first place.

Yet, I can't let him go through this alone.

HUDSON

I light up the sage, waving it up and down, and around my body to let the smoke hit my clothes and my skin. All for the sake of getting rid of the bad energy that's clinging to me.

"Please, go away," I grumble and stare at the smoke that's flowing away due to the wind.

Repeating the process one more time, I mutter, "That should do it," and let the sage drop down into the dirt.

I'm standing in front of the cabin I found in the forest two days ago. Instead of going home last night, I came here and spent the night. Whatever it is that's attached to me? I didn't want to have it follow me home and hurt my parents. I'm the one who brought it onto myself and I'm the one who has to deal with it.

After I played the game last night I freaked out and ran off when I heard someone coming up to the attic. It was stupid of me to forget to say goodbye. Such an easy thing to do and yet I simply got to my feet and let go of the planchette.

Ever since I left the attic I've been feeling weird. Like someone is following me around and is watching every step I take. I don't feel safe anymore. I've tried everything to shake it off, but nothing is working. I read online that people use sage for protection, and because I see Abbi sell crystals and other herbs, I thought I'd ask her and give it a try.

At this point I'm beyond desperate. I knew it was dangerous to play the game, but I was curious and dumb. I have no idea what this means for me, and how this is going to end. I do know that it's scaring the crap out of me that something is attached to me. And I have an eerie feeling I already know who it is.

Griffin, Artsy's father. A spirit that strong, who can show me what happened the night before, and has possessed me. He was the one I was talking to, so it has to be him. I can't let him hold that kind of power over me again. I need to remember who I am, stay strong and in charge so he can't take over my body.

But the bad thing is, I have no experience with things like this. I have zero idea how to undo or fix it. I didn't sleep at all last night. I see shadows everywhere, hear whispers, people calling my name, and even feel something touching my arm, or grabbing my ankles. This morning I nodded off and a burning pain woke up. Then I noticed a little scratch on my ankle of a nail, like someone tried to grab me and failed.

Did I mention I was damn stupid? I know for sure that this man, this thing, following me is evil. When he showed me what he did when he possessed me. The look on Artsy's face and the pain she was in? Horrifying. I just know it's not going to leave me alone until it gets what it wants.

What it is? I have no clue. Everything is freaking me out and I need to think clearly in an effort to remember crucial parts. I need to figure it out, but how am I going to do that if all I can see is the eyes that are staring at me from across the room in the dark corner. Am I hallucinating it or is it real? I have no damn clue.

I sigh. Completely sleep deprived I let myself drop back onto the bed. Shit. I can't ignore this thing. I have to face it head-on if I want to get rid of him. Gritting my teeth, I drag my tired body back up to glare at the eyes in the corner that are still staring at me.

"I will find a way to push you back into hell," I growl and fist my hands in my lap.

Nothing happens. No changes at all. Filled with frustration I take my head in my hands and close my eyes. I have to focus if I want to drag any piece of memory out of my brain that might help me fix this situation. There's a damn demon, a spirit, or whatever entity here with me I have to get rid of.

I try to remember what it was like when I was in the attic, roaming over the details in an effort to find a memory that might trigger something that might help me. My ears start to ring and I catch a glimpse of Griffin. I hold on to that memory and concentrate harder to make it last, hoping I can experience it all again.

I'm staring at Artsy. Griffin is telling her things through me, my hands are gripping the rose, the thorns biting into my skin. He's lashing out at her with words, making her bleed out of her eyes. Griffin is threatening her, telling her that she is a witch, a monster. Something about her not deserving to be alive.

I can feel his hatred flowing through me. The angry words he's telling her, lashing out, gripping the rose and ripping off the petals one by one. She's screaming. My own eyes are burning with unshed tears. The hate is intense and is burning me up from the inside out.

Tears are now spilling for what Artsy had to endure. The things he told her about her mother, what her father did, what she witnessed all those years ago. Then for him to tell her how she's just as much of a monster as her mother was. How she has to die as well. My heart shatters at the tormenting flashes of memory that are slicing through my brain.

I can't imagine how it must have been like for Artsy. No wonder Artsy threw me out that night. She was protecting herself, and me along with it. The things she had to endure, what she went through all those years…the bullying of me and my friends on top of it, and what happened when her father possessed me. I feel horrified and damn guilty.

Hearing Artsy ask what she did wrong, what her mom ever did to him, and why her father hates her so much is devastating. More flashes of memories flow through my head and the words "kill me" scream though my skull so loud, it hurts my ears. It doesn't stop me from trying to remember more. I have a feeling I'm close to finding out crucial details.

Griffin is talking about the flower, the one I saw in the attic. He's rattling how if someone kills the flower, two people will die. The one connected to it, and the one who destroyed it. Cursed. The rose and Artsy are cursed and don't belong in this world. Artsy is breaking apart. Not only due to her father harming the rose, but his words slice through her as well. She believes everything he says, I can clearly see it in her eyes.

The last petal is now between my fingers. It might just be a memory, but I can feel how velvety it is to the touch. Griffin is possessing me and in control of my body. He's ready to rip it off to end everything. Artsy suddenly realizes her father is possessing me.

The load of information Griffin threw at her is making sense. Her father killed her mother. That's why they are both dead. Griffin dies because he was the one who destroyed the rose. The curse. It's real. By killing his wife he passed it on to his daughter. That's how he died and found out he was cursed, and now he wants to kill Artsy because he blames her.

After all these years he's still trying to destroy the flower. How is he capable of doing that when he's dead? Is it part of the curse? Does his spirit linger or feed on revenge? Is there something keeping him linked to this world? If so, I need to find it and end this once and for all.

I raise my head and blink a few times to get rid of the blurry vision. The things I forced myself to remember are a lot to process. I should write everything down so I don't forget and try to make sense of everything. I have to make a plan to fix all of this. Even if I feel completely out of my depth.

I have no idea what I'm pulling myself into, but I'm in too deep already. At this point I'm either losing my mind, or facing things head on. Because getting ready to fight a demon doesn't sound like a reality, or the best plans for that matter. Yet, I'm committed when it comes to Artsy, and I owe it to her to fix it.

I grab some paper and a pencil out of my backpack and start to write down all the things I remember. There are whispers flowing around me. Voices screaming at me. They are hard to ignore, but I have to push through. The sooner I can come up with a plan, the sooner I can get rid of all of it.

For all I know he might be watching what I am doing, and knows I am trying to set it free. I might piss him off because he doesn't want freedom; it's revenge he's after. But I already faced and accepted the fact that I am putting myself in danger by doing this. I've seen enough movies and read up about these things last night to know that once you start, you can't go back. So, I'm seeing this through to the bitter end.

I glance at my phone and notice the time. I've spent over an hour brainstorming to come up with a plan. My phone is useless again. The cell service is spotty at best, and I can't seem to use a search engine right now to find some more answers.

If I thought I was feeling bad earlier, it's nothing compared to how I feel now. The need to throw up is huge, and my head is pounding as if I'm being hit by a sledgehammer every damn second. I bet Griffin has something to do with it. The eyes in the corner have morphed into his face, and he's been watching me the entire time while I was writing down my notes.

At first when I hightailed it out of the attic and rode off to the forest, I was terrified of him. I parked my bike and ran to the cabin, completely freaked out. I cried and screamed at every shadow I saw and each voice I heard. As the hours pass I am getting used to it. The pain, the terror, the agonizing torment he's putting me through. I don't think it can get any worse.

Yet, I'm no expert so he could easily be wearing me out while he's slowly growing in power by tormenting and clinging to me.

Every time I try to write something down, my eyelids fall shut and I start to drift off. I know my body is in dire need of some sleep and energy. But I can't, I have to stay awake. Who knows what might happen when I become unconscious with Griffin in the room. I am managing myself when I'm awake, but sleeping without knowing what is going on around me? No thanks. For all I know he could jump right into my body and possess me again.

I get to my feet and start to pace as I glance at the scattered papers that contain all my notes. I've highlighted some of my words with different colors, adding more notes. At least writing everything down and trying to come up with a plan did help me to stay focused instead of losing myself in the insanity of it all.

Though, every lead takes me back to the attic. If I want it to end, it has to happen in that place; where everything started.

I grab some of the papers and sit down. I have to go over everything again, keep myself busy so I won't fall asleep. Though, as I stare down, the letters start to swarm and my eyelids get heavy. Sleep is pulling me under and I have no other choice but to give in.

A HEART DOOMED BY FATE

ARTSY

I think I've been wandering this forest for a little over an hour. I never thought it would be this hard to find a cabin in the middle of nowhere, but I guess life keeps surprising me at every turn.

Meanwhile Mother Nature decides to throw in some more snow to add cold to the list of my complaints. I wish I was near a fire and had some hot cocoa in my hands. The memories of yesterday when I spent the day with Hudson assault me.

Sometimes I think about how my life would've been if I was like any other girl. No parents who died, no restrictions or extra care due to the rose that's linked to my life. My complete background wouldn't hang in the balance of the way I live. Things would be so different. I would be happy without a care in the world.

Ugh. Everyone has issues, even if all seems grand, it's due to bystanders looking into a picture-perfect life. Yet, I wouldn't be dealing with unexplainable shit, spirits, my dead mother still in my life through the reflection in the mirror.

I certainly wouldn't be wandering the woods, searching for the guy who bullied me for years. My crush who I opened myself up to and connected with on an intimate level. He's become so much more at rapid pace.

Fishing my phone out of my pocket, I check my messages to see if Hudson has read or replied. No service. Just great. If something bad happens, I wouldn't be able to call for help. Why did Hudson decide to run off into some cabin in the middle of the woods?

The only thing that would make sense is that something awful happened last night and that he can't be around people. Because that's where we are now. I shove my phone back into my pocket and come to a stop at a small clearing with a wooden cabin. This must be it.

I jog toward the cabin and stumble on the debris littering the ground. It looks completely abandoned. There's no way someone lives here on a regular basis. Should I knock? It doesn't look like anyone would answer, but there might be someone hiding in there. Hopefully not a serial killer.

Shit. This is stupid. I raise my fist to knock, but decide against it and grip the door handle instead. Slowly opening the door, I step inside and let it fall shut behind me to keep the snow and the cold outside. I notice someone standing in the middle of the room. Fear grips my heart and I realize this definitely wasn't a bright idea to come here alone.

Green eyes slowly glide in my direction. "Artsy?" he says with a hoarse voice.

"Hudson?" My jaw drops.

I found him. Abbi was right, he looks horrible. Eyes red with dark smudges underneath from lack of sleep, his hair a mess, clothes rumpled.

"Are you okay?" I ask with worry tainting my voice as I take a step in his direction.

"Peachy," he murmurs and sways on his feet.

He's lying. I'm pretty sure he hasn't slept all night and has been running around all morning, freaked out by the look on his face, and he's in this rundown cabin of all places.

"You look horrible," I state, and hear the cold wind howl around the cabin.

He sidesteps and mutters, "Oh."

Knocking himself off-balance, he starts to crumble to the floor and I barely manage to rush forward to protect his head from hitting the bedframe. He's too big for me to catch him, but at least I prevented a head injury.

My stomach drops and I snap, "Holy shit, that was close."

"Thanks," he mumbles and closes his eyes as if he's finally given in and is ready to take a nap.

"Yeah, you're welcome." I release a deep sigh, relieved he didn't hit his head. "You didn't have any sleep at all, did you?"

I slide my fingers through his blond hair, and he leans into my touch as he slowly shakes his head. Shifting his body he leans in and drops his head into my lap. I hope he's okay. I have no clue what's going on inside his head but there are no answers I can pull from his mouth with the state he's in.

This is all my fault. My past has put him in this state.

Guilt hits me hard. "It's okay, I'm here now," I whisper and try to swallow down the emotions that are clogging my throat.

Sitting on the floor, leaning my back against the bed, I simply stare at Hudson who is now sleeping in my lap. There's a snowstorm building outside by the sound of it, and I'm thankful to be here with him, safely out of the cold. I have no clue what to do, though. How did the two of us get pulled into this mess? Well, it's mostly; how do we get out of it.

"I tried to warn you," I muse as I stare at his sleeping face. "You couldn't leave it alone, could you?"

Sliding my thumb gently over his cheek, I feel tears well as they spill over. I only have myself to blame for putting his life on the line. I shouldn't have picked up the note he dropped for me to find. If I didn't follow him into that classroom, we wouldn't have ended up at my place again.

Why is he so persistent? Is it because of me? What drives him to follow me and meddle in my life, taking on issues that aren't his to deal with. And what does my father want with him? Possessing his body to come after me. Though, sitting here staring at a sleeping Hudson won't get me any answers.

I take a deep breath and grab one of the pillows from the bed to shove beneath Hudson's head so I can slide out from underneath him. Hudson is in a deep sleep and I can't wake him up. It's clear he won't let himself fall asleep by the state he was in. He needs it, though, and I'm here to watch over him.

I slide my hands around his body and with some pulling and shoving I barely manage to get his body up onto the bed so he can sleep comfortably. He needs his rest and after a few hours I'll wake him up so we can talk.

"That wasn't what I was expecting when I went out looking for him," I murmur to myself and glance around the room.

It's a complete mess. There are papers scattered all over the floor. They look like notes and I recognize Hudson's handwriting. Curiosity gets the better of me and I scoop up one of the notes to glance it over.

"The plan," I read softly out loud, not willing to wake Hudson.

I slide my finger over the note, checking the skin of my thumb after. A blue liquid is printed on my finger.

My thumb brushes over the words and I notice by the blue on the tip of my finger that this was recently written. I glance down at all the other scattered notes. Is this what he's been doing while he was hiding out here? I have to read all of them to see what he's been up to.

Maybe it will give me some answers, or at least make some sense as to why he's been up in the attic. He's sleeping for now and won't notice if I roam through his things if I keep quiet. Squatting down I reach for all the notes and try to read them one by one. Every word I read shocks me. There's so much information, confessions, answers.

When I get to the last note there's a word that shocks me. "Demon." That's what he's written down as if it's a conclusion. My eyes are wide when I let all the papers in my hand flow down onto the floor. What did I just read? Every word felt like a rollercoaster of things I didn't even know he was aware of.

He's in so much danger. If I believe the words he wrote on these papers, than that means that there is a demon in this cabin with us right now. And not just a random demon, or an evil spirit because of some dumb reason…no…it's my own father.

Hudson is sure of the fact that he thinks my father is a demonic spirit. One who is trying to break the curse tied to him, and the only way is to kill me like he did with my mother. His notes also contain an entire plan and it's scaring me how much Hudson already knows. He's found out way more than I have.

I have to talk to him when he wakes up. If he is right, then it means we have a very dangerous road ahead of us. Parts of his notes were gibberish and I think it's because of his lack of sleep. I couldn't make sense of it and I do hope he can when he wakes up, or at least remembers what he was trying to say.

I get to my feet and stalk to the chair in the corner to take a seat. I'm going to stay awake and watch over Hudson so he can gather his strength. Then, when he wakes up we can discuss all of this. For now I will make sure no demon will harm him. I know deep down that everything Hudson wrote in those notes is true. Everything makes sense.

He wrote down how Griffin, my father, followed him after playing the Ouija board. Not so surprising because I saw he didn't say goodbye by placing the planchette on those letters. He basically allowed my father to cling to him by doing that.

If only I knew how to fix all of this. I've been trying to make sense of it all for years since my mom passed. Even if I'm able to speak to my mom through her reflection, it's not like she reached out. I have no idea what happened to her, and nothing about her is mentioned in Hudson's notes either.

I guess I just have to wait for Hudson to wake up to get some answers. If he is telling the truth that is. I don't know who to trust anymore. Maybe Hudson's possessed, just like the time my father had a hold of him in the attic. Maybe this is just another trick of my father to get my attention, leading me right into one of his traps. My stress level is spiking just thinking about it.

I just don't get it. Why is my father using Hudson? Out of all people, why him? It's not making any sense. Minutes pass while my mind is going over all the options of what might be going on between my father and Hudson. Time passes and thankfully the storm has settled outside. My gaze shifts from the window to Hudson who is tossing and turning in his sleep.

His eyes are closed when he suddenly slides to the end of the bed. The way he's suddenly jerked down? There's no way he's doing it himself. It looks as if someone grabbed his ankles and pulled him to the edge of the bed. My heart sinks as I remember Hudson's notes. He clearly wrote that Griffin was following him everywhere. Is my father doing this?

I jump out of the chair and yell, "Hudson." He doesn't respond and I up my voice. "Hudson wake up."

I can see his eyes bounce left and right under his eyelids, and his body starts to shake as if he's having a seizure. No, no, no. I can't lose him.

"Wake up," I snap and grip his shoulders in an effort to snap him out of it.

As soon as my hand connects with his skin I'm hit with a jolt of what feels like electricity. Pain shoots up my arm and I step back by the force of it. My eyes widen and a chill runs up my spine. What the hell just happened? I feel a draft flowing around us. Is the demon Hudson mentioned present?

Hudson blinks and slowly awakes. "What?" he croaks.

"Are you okay?" I stare at him with wide eyes.

He's half draped over the bed and is slowly shifting into a sitting position.

"Yeah, I guess. Why, what happened?" He frowns and rubs his eyes.

"You didn't feel like someone was grabbing you?" I question, my heart still racing at the very thought of what I just witnessed.

His frown is still in place. "No. I just woke up from the sound of your voice."

He shakes his head and looks at me, confusion filling his face. I'm still freaking out. How did he not feel it? Hell, my mind can't even wrap around the fact that something…someone…a damn spirit or demon grabbed him and tried to yank him off the bed. I guess my father is either very powerful or he's in some way feeding off of Hudson's energy or something.

"I swear what happened isn't normal. I saw with my own eyes how something, someone, grabbed you by the ankles and tried to pull you off the bed." I choke out the words and scan the room as if any second something could attack us.

Though I don't see anything or anyone.

"You're joking?" I can tell he's trying to make light of the situation, but I can clearly see the concern written all over his face.

"No, this is not a damn joke. I swear I saw it happen with my own damn eyes, Hudson," I growl, trying to make him understand how serious this is.

"I knew I had to stay awake." He drops his head in his hands. "I wasn't aware I'd fallen asleep. What are you even doing here?" he grumbles and gives me a weary look.

"I went into the attic and saw that someone had played the Ouija board. I knew it had to be you, no one else was in the house and I knew my grandparents wouldn't step foot in the attic. I want an explanation," I snap. "But I think I already know." I point at the scattered notes on the floor.

"You read those?" Hudson sneers, as if he caught me doing something I wasn't supposed to do.

"Yes, I did. You need to explain to me what you think is happening, and how we can stop this. Because I have no idea what happened to my mother, and how you even know all of this. For years I've been trying to figure it out, suddenly you enter my life and have all these details that I didn't even know about," I screech in an accusing tone.

"I have no idea myself, Artsy," he growls back.

"Why are you angry at me? I tried to keep you away and created distance between us, but it was you who forced yourself back into my life. So, don't you dare yell at me. I watched over you so you could get some sleep and I woke you up when I thought someone was trying to hurt you and then you lash out? You're an asshole, Hudson," I snarl, anger burning hot in my veins.

He takes a deep breath and visibly calms himself before he says, "I'll explain everything to you. I made a plan, but I do need your help to pull it off."

"Well, I guess that depends," I huff, still not trusting any of this.

What I just witnessed freaked me out and I'm not sure about Hudson's motivation either. For all I know he could be working with my father. I've seen Hudson getting possessed by him before, so who knows? My father could still be using him to get what he wants.

"C'mon. Don't you want to talk to your mom again, and get rid of your father? We also need to end the curse that was passed down from your mother to you. Which is also the reason why your father wants to kill you," Hudson says, triggering me with all the reasons why I'm here in the first place.

There isn't any other option but to agree to work with him. Even if it might cost me my own life.

"Fine," I huff. "But if I think you're full of shit and are working against me instead of with me, then I'll drop you like a hot potato and you'll leave me alone once and for all," I tell him.

Of course I want everything to end, and everything back to normal. Well, as normal as it can be. Though, right now I have no clue what normal is. I just want all of the craziness to end.

"I promise you my plan will be worth it," Hudson promises, and snags one of the papers from the ground.

It's the one that didn't make sense to me, the handwriting is awful and it's all gibberish.

"Weird," he mutters and raises his eyebrow as he stares at the paper.

"What's weird?" I ask.

"Look at it," he states and jabs the piece of paper in my direction.

I let my gaze roam over the paper. It's still not making any sense to me. "What about it? It's like it's been written by a six-year-old and it's not making any sense at all."

I shake my head, not understanding what he's getting at. If this is all he's going to say or do, then I'm just wasting my time here.

"No, you dumbass. Look at the writing," he insists and is clearly angry that I don't get what he's saying.

At first I thought he was still tired, but I can clearly see the frustration written on his face. The cold draft wraps around us again and I shiver at the reminder of a presence being here with us. What is Hudson trying to say?

A HEART DOOMED BY FATE

CHAPTER 18

HUDSON

How is she not seeing what I'm seeing? It's so damn clear, I have the proof in my hands. Dammit, she saw someone grabbing me by the ankle, and now this. There is no way she can't deny what is happening here.

"I didn't write it like this," I snap and wave the note in front of her. "I didn't suddenly change my handwriting or fall asleep while writing." Her eyes widen as I try to explain everything.

I can tell she's afraid with the wide eyes and the step back she's taking. Her chest rises and falls and her hand slowly moves to cover her mouth.

"The scary part is, this is the only note that had my actual plan on it. It's not a damn coincidence that the only piece that had the possible solution to get rid of him is now ruined. The only note. Unreadable. Like it doesn't want us to figure it all out." I'm explaining it all to her while my mind is jumping all over the place in an effort to figure things out.

Sadly there's not much to figure out since I was sleeping when it happened. The only other person who was in here was Artsy and she's mad as hell about everything. There's no way she did anything so that leaves the spirit of her father who could have ruined it.

"He is scared," Artsy states and she bobs her head.

She's right. If he did in fact ruin the note where I wrote down the plan it might just have been a way to get rid of him. He knows we're onto him and are finding a way to make him leave our world.

"He is. All the time I spent with him, and the hours I forced myself to remember everything I've been trying to find out what he's doing here. What it is he wants and how he wants to do it. I have a plan to send him back. So, if you finally believe me, do you trust me enough to help me?" I ask.

I hope to hell she says yes because I cannot do it without her help. There are some things I have no clue about and she might have the missing details. The only way this will work is if we work together.

She bobs her head. "Let's do it." Her voice is firm and her steps are determined as she gets into my personal space and snatches the note from my hand. "Tell me how."

"Okay let's start at the beginning," I tell her.

It's best we go over everything together to fill in the gaps.

"When Griffin possessed me, he went straight for the rose and wanted to destroy it. He used it to get answers from you and manipulated you with his lies. Your mother died because Griffin found out the rose was connected to her. He thought the love between them was fake, that it was all a lie due to the influence of the rose." I shake my head and remember the things I researched and pieced together before I fell asleep. "The flower itself is defined as a symbol for love. But then again, a black rose defines death. The combination of black and red, him finding out about the rose that runs in your family, the life of the owner connected to it… he thought the only way to break the connection, and destroy the rose was to–"

"Kill their love," she finishes for me, realization written all over her face.

"Exactly. In his mind the only reasonable explanation for his feelings toward your mother. He felt cheated and deemed her a monster for being connected to the rose. Not understanding led to him thinking you were witches, poisoning life and love while cursing others and rob them of their hearts and lives. And what is the only way to get rid of a haunted or cursed object?" I question, letting her connect the dots.

"To destroy it," she muses with a frown on her face.

I nod. "So, the night he killed your mother, he went into the attic and grabbed the glass bowl protecting it and grabbed the flower. He rushed downstairs to confront your mother. I've seen it through his eyes. He let me see what he did when he possessed me, but he also gave me a look into his mind about that crucial night all those years ago. I felt the thorns stab into his skin and mine when he started to pull off every single petal. I saw the look on your mother's face when her own husband killed her.

Saw the look of love turn to shock, horror, and fear."

I take a moment to let her process the information before I continue. "He explained his idiotic reasoning while ripping the petals. How she tricked him, that nothing between them was real. He thought he was saving the world and gaining back the freedom she stole from him by putting him under her spell. Your mother stayed quiet through it all. Through his eyes I saw how she bled from her eyes the way you did that night in the attic. The pain he caused. She took it all until the last petal fell. Only then she told him that he wouldn't survive either if he killed her. But he already ripped off the last petal, sealing both their fate. By killing her, he released the curse of the flower, and passed it on to his own daughter. He killed his wife, himself, and pulled you into the same path. He only has himself to blame, and yet all he's still thriving on is revenge."

Artsy glances up to me. Her hands are shaking and tears are rolling down her cheeks. I can't blame her. Her past and present have collided. Losing both parents is horrifying, but having them ripped from her the way it happened, and having her father coming after her to kill her as well is insane to say the least.

"Your father couldn't handle unhuman circumstances. If he'd left the rose alone nothing would have happened. He might have been afraid, didn't understand it, and thought he was doing the right thing, maybe even did it to protect you. In the end, everything escalated and now you're in the same situation. Their death transferred everything onto you, so now his revenge is fully focused to end you. That's why you kicked me out of the house, right? When he possessed me he filled your head with all these lies. How it's the curse that links us, that our hearts are connected through the rose and that I will do the same once we grow close. He's wrong, Artsy."

I step closer and reach out to gently brush her tears from her cheek with my thumb. "His own actions and thoughts drove him to it. You and I? We didn't simply fall in love. Our paths crossed a long time ago and we collided a different way. I was your bully so how's that love, eh? No curse would ever let anyone fall in love that way. Yes, I noticed you, but there was no swoon-worthy moment. I hated seeing you get hurt by others and that made us have a normal discussion. We talked. We spent time together. That's how normal people fall in love. Everything else we can deal with as long as we believe what works for us. Screw the rose or the curse for that matter. It's only important because we need to get rid of your father's spirit who is trying to kill you and isn't afraid to use me to get his way."

She leans into my touch and has her fingers gripping the front of my shirt when she says, "So what can we do to stop him?"

"We have to go back to the attic and play his game. Something is missing, I just know it. I remember writing it down, but all the words are smudged. We have to figure it out all over again." I release a frustrated sigh that I can't remember that part anymore while most things are now clear. "We need to play the Ouija board."

Just the thought of doing it gives me chills. Artsy shakes her head and steps back.

There's a load of venom in her voice when she snaps, "No. No way."

"We have to. We're out of options here, Artsy. He still holds all the answers and I'm guessing we need to help your mother too, right?" I know I'm grasping at straws here, but maybe she'll agree when it involves her mother as well.

I'm not liking this either, but what else can we do except go all in. Running away won't help a damn thing.

She nibbles on her bottom lip and suddenly mutters, "I have another idea."

"Which is?" I wonder.

"I have a way to contact my mom and we could do that before we go into the attic. She might know the answers to some of the questions we have. She can definitely tell us more about the rose, and why it's in my family," she suggests and shoots a look over her shoulder.

"I thought your mother's reflection left the mirror after I started played the board?" I rub the back of my neck, trying to understand what she means.

"How do you know about that?" Her eyes go wide when her head whips my way again, concern visible on her face.

"Uh, that's kinda the reason why I was playing the Ouija board." I groan. "It's a long story."

"Alright?" She shrugs as if to tell me we have all the time in the world.

We keep staring at one another until she turns and points at where she was looking earlier. "I know a way to contact her from in here."

I glance that way and notice that she's pointing out the mirror.

"Why would she come here?" I wonder.

Her gaze wanders through the cabin. "Because I now recognize this place."

I'm the one frowning now and ask, "You recognize this cabin?"

She turns and steps closer to the mirror. "I think this is the cabin my grandfather built when my mother was a little girl. She always took her dog with her when she helped my grandfather and they would play in the forest as well. I'm surprised it's still here. I remember my grandmother showing me pictures of my mother and her dog. I've never been here, though." She touches the chair in the corner. "I remember this chair in one of the pictures."

"Do you think she still comes around here because she used to come here as a kid?" I question.

"I guess." Artsy shrugs as she stares at the mirror.

"That makes sense why she popped up in this mirror and spoke to me," I whisper, mainly to myself.

Though, Artsy heard it too because she gasps. "You spoke to my mom?"

"Yeah. Remember the night you kicked me out? The weather was horrible and I wandered through the forest and found this cabin where I took shelter. She spoke to me and offered me a deal. I really wanted to know what happened during the time where there's a gap in my memory, so I accepted but everything got a little out of hand," I explain and sit down on the floor next to her.

"But how can you see her? I'm the only one who is able to talk to and see her because I was there when she died," she murmurs in confusion.

"I have no clue. Maybe because I was possessed by her husband? It might have given me some kind of connection to the paranormal side or something? Who knows. Just thinking about the why and how gives me the creeps." I shiver.

Artsy slowly bobs her head. "Now that you mention it, that does make sense."

"Why don't you take lead?" I offer.

I mean, it's her mom and after what happened the last time I talked to her, I'm not looking forward to any of this paranormal shit. If anything, I can still feel a presence here with us. For all we know her father is listening in on us and knows exactly what we're up to.

"Mom, are you here? We want to ask you something important, if that's okay," Artsy says.

A few breaths later there's a woman appearing in the mirror in front of us. It's the same woman I talked to as well.

"Hey, Mom," Artsy quips with fondness in her voice.

I turn to look at Artsy. Her whole face has gone soft with affection when she looks at her mother. It's clear she feels safe and happy to know that her mom is here with her, even if it's just a reflection. I can feel a smile slide across my face and I turn in the direction of the mirror again to see the reflection of the three of us together.

"He's here," her mother growls.

"I know. I'm sorry. Some things went wrong, and we are working on fixing all of it. But we need your help," I rattle before Artsy can say anything else.

"You failed," her mother huffs.

"No, I didn't! I had no idea what was going on," I snap in frustration.

I have to stay calm. Throwing angry words back and forth isn't going to help our situation. I take a deep breath and try to catch my bearings.

"We know a way, trust me. But for our plan to fall together we need to know why the flower is in our family. We have to make sense of it all to be able to connect the dots," Artsy says, taking over the conversation.

"It's a long story," her mother states and crosses her arms in front of her chest.

Artsy shrugs. "We have time."

"Very well." She sighs and points at us. "Maybe you remember this cabin from the pictures in your grandparents' photo album. I grew up around here. My father built this cabin and when I was younger I loved gardening and planting flowers. Me and my family went to the market to buy seeds. One time I caught sight of a black flower with red lines across the petals. I knew right away I wanted it. I begged my father to buy it for me, and he did."

Her eyes drift down and she frowns. "It was like my mind was drawn to it. I couldn't stop thinking about that rose and how special it was. I wanted to go to it all the time, touch it, smell it, stare at it, sleep beside it, do my homework close to it, and spend all my free time near that flower. My father was getting worried and paid a visit to the man he bought it from. He wanted to know what was going on and if it was some kind of special flower. When he returned home, he obviously found me with the rose. But this time, I pulled the flower out and held it in my hands."

She shakes her head and stares at us with sadness on her face. "He was shocked and couldn't believe his eyes. Blood was dripping from my hands because the thorns cut through my skin. I couldn't feel the pain because of my obsession with the flower. My father tried to take the flower from me, telling me how the previous owner had no idea what kind of rose it was. The man just needed money so he sold the flower. I had no idea why my father was so worried. I didn't think there was anything wrong. I pulled a petal from the rose and quickly shoved it into my mouth, swallowing it down. Don't ask me why, because I don't know why I ate the petal, I just felt the need to do it. It was harmless, but instantly I started feeling sick. My father tried to get rid of the rose, but I managed to hide it in the attic and kept it covered with a glass bowl so it wouldn't hurt anyone."

A tear leaves her eye and I feel sorry for her. The story is personal, and I never expected the background story to be so innocent. A child's interest in flowers turned dangerous through a special kind of rose she ran into.

"Without realizing what I'd done, the rose attached itself to me. Every time something happened to the flower, I would get a sharp pain in my chest, as if my heart was getting crushed. There was no other choice but to keep it. Years passed and then I met your father, then we had you. The rose stayed in the attic over time, and I never thought about it again until your father found it one day. I freaked out when he removed the bowl and angrily told him to never come near it, that it was a part of me. I guess his imagination got the better of him. I had a bad feeling about all of it, though I never expected him to deliberately destroy the rose so he could destroy me." Her last words fade away, as does she when it's just the two of us left in the reflection of the mirror.

A HEART DOOMED BY FATE

ARTSY

"So, now what?" I hear Hudson ask beside me.

I slowly turn my head to face him. "I have no idea."

My mind is still reeling from what my mother just explained. Such a simple act with huge changes that impact all of our lives.

"At least we know the background story," he quips.

"Maybe," I muse and get to my feet.

"What do you mean, maybe? Your mom explained everything that happened to us." He frowns and stands.

"Yes, we heard my mom's story. But not my father's side of it. Maybe he knows more, something my mother never knew." I rub my temples. "Don't you think it's weird that my father finds the rose in the attic and suddenly goes ballistic and destroys it? Who does that? Wouldn't there be more explanation? Reasons? I just feel that there's something missing. Someone doesn't scream witch or curse or rip up a rose knowing you're hurting someone. Especially not the person you spent years with, married, and have a kid with. I'm telling you, something is missing. I have a feeling my father knows something no one else does."

"We need to find the person who sold the rose to your grandfather. Do you think it's possible to ask him about it?" Hudson questions and brushes the dust off his knees.

I sigh. "It's worth a shot I guess. Though, I don't think he will remember."

I feel nauseous talking about all of this.

"Okay, let's go to your house first and ask him about it. If that doesn't work, we know what to do," he states and stalks to the bed to grab his backpack.

"Do what?" I whisper, knowing very well what he has in mind.

"Play the game so we can contact your father to get some answers," he simply says.

A chill runs up my spine at the very thought. I just hope my grandpa still knows who sold him the flower, or anything else he can tell us about it. I really don't want to play any game, especially one that involves a Ouija board, or talking to my father for that matter.

It's a bit strange that when we talked to my mom, not a single thing happened. Hudson didn't get grabbed, there were no voices or strange sounds, or anything else. Almost as if my mother's presence kept my father at a distance.

"Let's go," Hudson quips and holds the door open for me.

The cold wind assaults us and luckily it's stopped snowing. We're heading to my grandparents' house and luckily Hudson knows exactly what path to take. We're walking for a few minutes when Hudson winces and shoots a quick glance over his shoulder.

"Something wrong?" I whisper, and already know I won't like his answer by the look on his face.

"He's following us," Hudson whispers back.

I glance over my shoulder as well but don't see anything out of place.

There's no need to ask who "he" is so instead I grunt, "Are you sure?"

"Yeah," he replies with a shaky voice, and adds, "He has been following us the entire time."

"How do you know? Can you see him?" I wonder, turning around to walk backwards to see what he's seeing, but there's nothing there.

Hudson shakes his head. "No, not really. It's more like I can feel his presence."

I shiver. I am glad it's not me experiencing that. I would freak out if I felt someone watching me at every turn. Let's hope my grandfather remembers something from all those years ago so we have a clue or a lead to check out and get rid of all of this once and for all.

Hudson reaches out and links his fingers with mine. "Come on, let's hurry up."

The both of us are uncomfortable walking through the forest with someone following us. Darkness is closing in and that doesn't make it any less eerie either.

"Agreed," I muse and we pick up our pace.

I practically jump out of my skin when I hear a noise behind us. I quickly whip my head around to make sure no one is coming after us. Except, there's nothing there, just trees. I release a shaky breath.

Glancing up at Hudson I grumble, "I can't do this."

My voice is shaking and my nerves are all over the place. Why is my life so complicated and took a turn to complete havoc? Demons, curses, angry spirits, as if there isn't enough personal stuff I get to deal with by taking classes and getting bullied. None of this makes sense and right now we don't have a solution to fix whatever this is. Hell, if we even can fix it, because that too isn't guaranteed.

"It's going to be okay, I promise," Hudson firmly states and brings us to a stop so he can pull me into his strong arms. "I won't let him hurt you. I swear. I'm right here, Artsy. I'll protect you no matter what happens."

His lips are soft when he kisses me. My heart is racing inside my chest for a completely different reason now. How can he take away all my fears with a simple kiss? He makes me feel safe, as if we can face whatever comes our way together. I let his warmth fill my body and ground myself by fisting the fabric of his jacket to keep him close.

Nothing has changed about the situation we're in and yet the understanding that I'm not alone anymore gives me the strength to continue to fight. He pulls back all too soon and places his forehead against mine, the gesture intimate and loving.

"Let's do this," he tells me and his determination is boosting my motivation as well.

I bob my head and we continue the path in the direction of the house. The small talk we share, along with talking through some of the things we experienced in the attic, keeps the both of us focused.

After a few minutes we're in front of the house and Hudson rings the doorbell. My grandpa is the one who opens the door and he frowns when he notices me and Hudson.

"Why are you two outside? It's late, dark, and cold," he snaps and glares at the both of us.

Gramps is always a bit grumpy. I ignore his question and instead ask, "We're here because we need to ask you something important."

His face slides from grumpy to concern. "Is everything alright?"

"Not really, Gramps. Hudson and I found out a few things and there are some missing parts we'd really like to have answers to," I explain and jab my thumb in Hudson's direction.

Gramps frowns when he takes in Hudson. "Who is that? Did he hurt you?"

"No, he's my friend. No worries," I quickly tell him.

"Well, come inside then, we're letting out all the heat standing here talking." He steps back and allows us to enter the house.

Hudson closes the door behind us and we follow grandpa into the living room.

"Sit down," Gramps orders as he points at the couch. "What do you guys want to know?"

Hudson and I take a seat right next to each other.

I might as well get straight to the point. "Gramps, do you remember when my mother was little, and you bought her a black rose? One she couldn't stay away from? Do you know who sold you that flower?"

"Oh, young girl, that was a very long time ago." He leans back in his chair and yawns.

I place my forearms on my knees and lean forward. "I know, but it is really important."

He frowns and looks thoughtful when he says, "Well, I don't remember. It's been too long, but I'm fairly sure I still have the receipt somewhere in a box. Your mother made sure I didn't throw it away."

A spark of hope hits me. "Where is the box now, Gramps?"

He points at the ceiling. "It's up in the attic. I don't know exactly where, but it must be somewhere between all the other boxes."

My stomach drops. No, not the attic. The one place I don't want to be near at this time is exactly where we need to go. I glance at Hudson, who is already looking at me. Shit. There's no other way.

"Thanks," I tell grandpa and get to my feet.

He doesn't ask any questions as to why we're bringing it up. Instead he gives Hudson a smile as we stroll out of the room. I'm about to tell Hudson that we can't go up there when he dashes around me and runs up the stairs.

I quickly rush after him. "What do you think you're doing? Hudson! I am not going up to the attic. Hudson, don't ignore me, I know you can hear me, dammit."

I try to snatch him by his shirt when he whirls around. "Then you wait here, but I need to get rid of your demonic father who is following me around. He's already tried to harm you and is trying to hurt me as well because he's furious that we're getting closer to getting some damn answers."

I freeze at the harshness in his voice. He gives me a fierce stare while

I try to find words to say to him. I do understand the anger and frustration. Hell, I feel it too. Everything we've experienced in these past few days alone is terrifying and traumatizing. He even has a demonic spirit clinging to him…my father. Though, he didn't tell me my father is trying to hurt him. Everything was fine in the forest. What changed?

He takes a step to the door of the attic. "Are you coming or what?"

"I need to," I instantly reply.

It's not like I have a choice. It's my fault. If I would have pushed my mother to explain everything to me instead of just listening to her when she told me to protect the rose…maybe none of this would have happened. I should have researched everything and not listened to my mother to leave the past behind and focused on protecting myself; protecting the rose.

"Good," Hudson grunts and opens the door.

The Ouija board is still on the floor, surrounded by the candles. I can feel my eyes go wide. The candles are still burning? No. That can't be. They're thick candles, but it's been a full day since…and I killed the flames myself.

"You left the candles burning?" Hudson asks with a concerned look on his face.

"No way. They weren't lit when I left the attic after I didn't see anyone here last night. I swear I extinguished the candles myself," I whisper with a shaky voice.

The sight of the board along with the candles gives me the chills, let alone the knowledge that we didn't light the candles. Then who did? My grandparents wouldn't light candles up here, of that I'm certain.

"I think someone wants us to play." Hudson jerks his chin in the direction of the Quija board.

Did my father light the candles? My legs feel like Jell-O as I step closer to the Ouija board. I do hope we're not making the biggest mistake ever by doing this. I start to glance through the boxes in an effort to find the one my grandfather mentioned; the one with the receipt for the rose. It has to be here, and I won't be playing anything until I've found it.

A HEART DOOMED BY FATE

CHAPTER 20

HUDSON

I watch Artsy throw pieces of paper onto the floor. She's making a mess as she searches for the receipt. Swallowing hard, I glance around and have no clue what to do next. All of this freaks me out and I want to get it over with. Raw emotions are hitting me hard.

This is the place where I was possessed. Where I lost track of my own mind and had to see it by standing on the sidelines how I almost killed this wonderful girl. My girl. Even if I wasn't the one doing it, I still felt and experienced every moment of it.

I'm also the one who played the board and didn't say "Goodbye" to close the session. I'm the one the demonic spirit is clinging to. Every single moment is running through my brain. The moment I met Artsy, how I've bullied her for a long time.

All while she's been through horrific things herself and is still so very strong. Regret and guilt burn through my gut. I'm the one who also added to her pain by tormenting her at school. I never meant to hurt her. My chest is heaving while my mind is reeling.

"Hudson," Artsy snaps right in front of my face, ripping me out of my thoughts.

I give my head a quick shake. "Huh?"

"What are you doing?" she asks, concern sliding across her face.

My gut turns and I have to blink a few times as I rub my temples. "I don't feel so good."

This place is making me sick, or even worse…he is. Griffin. He's trying to get me out of here.

"All of this is messing with your head," Artsy states, concern clear in her voice.

She takes my hand and gives it a tiny squeeze before she shoves something in it. "I found something."

I glance at the card she placed in my hand, it looks like a business card.

"Do you think this is where they bought the flower?" I ask, letting my gaze collide with hers.

"It's a flower shop, so probably." She shrugs. "We can try calling the number, see if it's still active."

She points at the number on the bottom of the card.

"Let's try it," I agree, and fish my phone out of my pocket. "Maybe we should do it downstairs. I don't feel comfortable being here."

I don't wait for her to answer and stalk in the direction of the door.

"My room?" Artsy suggests, hearing her footsteps close behind me.

We descend the stairs and enter her room. She closes the door and I hand her the card and my phone.

She shakes her head and gently shoves my hand back. "Can you make the call? I'm too nervous."

She stalks away and sits down on her bed.

I'm just as stressed about this, but I've discovered that I would do anything for this girl. Handing her the card, Artsy reads the numbers out loud while I jab the screen of my phone. There's a weird feeling in my gut that gives me the impression that this call could either go good or really, really bad.

The line is silent and I mutter a soft, "Hello?"

There's a click and then a tape starts with a deep voice that dictates a message, "You've reached Rhine Burton flower store. I regret to inform you that my shop is now closed. Thank you for the support."

"And?" Artsy whispers eagerly.

Taking the phone away from my ear I frown and tell her, "There was a message that he closed the shop."

Her shoulders sag. "Did it say anything else?"

"Nope. The message was only the name of the shop and that they were closed, thanking the customers for their support, nothing else." I shove my phone back into my pocket and glance at my girl.

"What was the name of the store? Maybe we can search for more information online," Artsy asks.

"Rhine Burton." I feel a shiver pass through me when the name leaves my mouth.

Her eyes widen and her jaw drops.

"What? Do you know him?" I question, though her reaction is practically all the answer I need.

"Burton," she echoes.

"That is what I said, yes," I mumble, hoping she's going to spill more details as to why the name is so shocking.

"Griffin Burton," she croaks on a torn whisper.

The name slides through my head. No way. That can't be.

"Are you shitting me? That's your father's name? So, what? Your father's the son of the man who sold the rose to your grandpa?"

Now I can feel my own eyes widen.

She slowly nods, tears well up in her eyes and there's confusion filling her face. "I never met my grandparents from my father's side."

I take her hand to give her some comfort, but we can't dwell on this. We need answers and there's only one option left.

"There's no way around it, Artsy." I clear my throat and get to my feet. "We have to talk to your father."

Artsy rips her hand back and shakes her head. There's fear filling her gaze and I hate to be the one who put it there. I don't like it either, but we're running out of options.

"The sooner we do this, the faster we can put all of this behind us," I tell her, knowing it won't make a lick of difference to take away the stress and pressure.

I hardly believe the words I just gave her myself. Every second I think we're getting closer to unraveling this mystery, it feels as if we're taking a step back and getting farther away from the solution.

She stands and strides to the door without a single word.

"Artsy wait," I yell, but she doesn't stop.

She heads for the stairs and all I can do is follow her up until we step foot in the attic. Artsy whirls around to face me and points at the floor where the Quija board is.

"Let's do this," she practically growls with determination.

I nod, knowing the danger I am putting myself in again. The candles are already lit and the only thing we have to do is sit down so I can place my hands on the planchette. I sit down behind the board while Artsy sits down on the other side so I can stare into her eyes, giving me a hint of comfort.

"Ready?" I whisper while I let my hands hover above the board.

She glances at the mirror and murmurs, "Mom, please stay with me."

Her gaze connects with mine when she states, "Ready."

I take a gulp of air into my lungs and place two fingers on the planchette. Artsy reaches out and does the exact same thing.

"Follow my instructions," I tell her.

I know she's never done this before. I'm not an expert, but I've done this once before and above anything else, I want to appear as if I know my shit because she deserves as much through the havoc that's her life.

I move the planchette, making it spin in three full circles on the board.

"We are here to talk." My voice is loud and firm to make sure anyone in the room can hear me.

I wait to ask my first question until I feel a light breeze flow over my skin. This gives me the indication there's someone here with us.

"Griffin. We know you are the son of the man who sold the rose. Do you know why Artsy's mom was so obsessed with it?" I question, keeping my eyes on the board, waiting for him to reply by moving the planchette.

Slowly I feel movement underneath my fingers, guiding the planchette. Artsy's eyes widen as we watch it slide over the board.

Artsy leans forward and murmurs, "Yes," reading the word under the glass circle in the planchette.

Her gaze collides with mine and I know she's thinking the same thing as me; he knows what happened. He knew about the flower before he saw it in the attic.

"So, that means he had something to do with it, right?" I whisper to Artsy.

Her lips part, but she doesn't get a chance to reply when the planchette moves back and forth to cover the "yes" with the glass circle to answer my question. If he had something to do with it…then what did he do to the rose before his father sold it?

The man wasn't supposed to sell it, but Artsy's mother wanted it badly so her father offered a lot and the man needed money. What the hell happened to the rose?

"What did you do to the rose before it was sold?" Artsy asks and the planchette instantly starts to glide over the board to spell a string of letters.

I connect all the letters and state, "Poison." I frown and ask to clarify, "You poisoned the flower?"

The planchette moves back to the "yes" in the corner of the board. That's crazy. Why would he poison a rose that's in his father's flower shop? It doesn't make sense and somehow I think there's more to it than that. My gut tells me we're still missing pieces of the puzzle and we need to ask more questions.

"You should continue to ask questions," I tell Artsy. "I think he prefers talking to you."

She nods nervously. "Did you do it on purpose?"

Her voice is a little shaky. Not so weird because this is her father she's talking to, and it involves her mother's death, trying to unravel the why and how of the traumatic events in her past. The answers will either weigh heavy on her soul or give some relief to cope with all of it in the future.

I hold my breath while the planchette slides to the "no" on the board, and release it in a huff.

"That's good," I mutter in relief.

"That still doesn't make him an innocent in all of it," Artsy snaps and glances back at the board to ask her next question. "What happened? How do you poison a flower by accident?"

We watch how he points out letters and once done Artsy and I both state in sync, "Dropped."

Both of us are silent as we process the details we just found out.

I clear my throat and tell her, "Your father was a little kid when it happened. Maybe he was in his father's store playing around and accidentally knocked something off a table and it spilled on the flower?"

Our eyes stay on the board, but nothing happens.

"It still doesn't make sense, Hudson. Why would they own poison at a flower shop?" Artsy asks me. "Why would a parent let their child play in a store where they have poison out in the open?"

Shit, she's right. No sane parent would do that.

"But what other way is there for him to accidently drop poison onto a flower that's ready to be sold?" I frown.

"They were buying seeds," Artsy quips. "They weren't buying flowers, but seeds, that's when she noticed the flower. But that still doesn't answer the question as to why a flower shop would own poison, though."

Poison is also not something that would make a flower attach to someone or cause such a reaction.

"What did the jar of poison look like?" The random question falls from my lips because this happened when her father was just a kid.

Who knows what was in the bottle he spilled onto the flower and how it got there. This sure wasn't some random insecticide or whatever.

The planchette moves over the letters.

"Old," I murmur as I put them together.

Artsy gasps. "Holy shit, Hudson."

"What? Do you know something?" I ask and let my gaze hit hers.

"My father once told me that his grandparents used to own a spice shop. They mixed all kinds of spices and herbs to create potions, salves, pills, and stuff to cure wounds or treat health issues. I remember because he mentioned some clients came for potions to help slow down aging, that kind of weird stuff," she rattles.

"What does that have to do with poison and the flower?" I question, not understanding what link she's trying to make inside her head.

She groans. "He said the jar looked old, right? What if they took over the spice shop and turned it into a flower shop? Some of the old inventory might still have been lingering around and my dad found it as a kid. That would explain the poison and how he could have accidentally spilled it onto the flower."

"Yeah, that does make sense. Simple, harmless, an accident." I bob my head, feeling for the first time that every piece of the puzzle is sliding into place. "Then, after all those years, he sees the flower and confronts your mother. He must have panicked, wanting to destroy the flower because he knew it was poisonous. Your mother spilling the details how it's linked to her...the self-blame projected onto your mother...point of no return. Killing the flower to hide his own mistake killed them both," I ramble, understanding what happened that caused us to be here within this moment to unravel the history of Artsy's family.

The planchette moves to the corner of the board and confirms our ramblings when we both read "yes" through the round glass. We pieced it together. How can something so complicated all come down to one innocent mistake as a kid? The injustice is a strong factor in all of this, especially when it comes to Artsy. We might have found out about the why and how, but it still doesn't solve everything.

ARTSY

I am still shocked that we figured out my family's mystery. I can't believe I never made the link with my father's side of the family owning the spice shop. The answer to why and how was so easy and yet completely out of reach. It's also crazy that my mom never let me figure this out, or knew it was my father who spilled something on the rose to make it connect with her.

"We might have found out all these details about how the rose was cursed, but we still don't know how to remove the curse. My father's spirit is also still attached to you, and clearly the curse twisted his mind or something. Hell, maybe it's just an excuse I try to find for his actions, anger, revenge, whatever he's doing." I sigh and feel a little deflated, even if we've come so close to unraveling all of it.

"True. But maybe we can find that out as well," Hudson states and jerks his chin in the direction of the board.

"How can we get rid of the curse?" I blurt, and hope my father answers my question.

Except, the planchette stays in place.

I glance up at Hudson. "Why isn't it moving?"

Hudson shrugs. "Either Griffin left or he doesn't want to answer, or maybe he doesn't know."

I don't believe my father would leave. What we're revealing involves him as well. So, I'm guessing he either doesn't want to answer, or he doesn't know how to get rid of the curse. There's also a possibility that he doesn't want to remove the curse, but that he wants to end it all. Could he really be consumed by revenge all these years? Or maybe he forgot it was an accident when he became a spirit?

I have no clue about his state of mind, or what he wants. The last time he tried to kill me. Then again, what if his mind was tainted by the rose as well because he was holding it when my mother found him with it in the attic?

As a kid he also didn't know what kind of poison was in the jar. He only said it looked old. How would he know if there even was a cure when he was a kid when it happened and the contents of the jar were old.

"Artsy." Hudson's voice draws me out of the ramblings of my mind.

"Hm?" I mumble.

"This might sound like a dumb suggestion…but…remember how your mom explained to us that she ate a petal from the flower because she was so drawn to it and all? Well, by eating the petal the curse entered her body. Did you ever try eating one of the petals?" Hudson asks, his voice a bit unsure.

I can feel my eyes widen. "No, of course I never tried to eat it. The thought never occurred to me. It's not like I was obsessed with the rose the way my mother explained it to us when she got it. When my mother died she told me go live with my grandparents. My rose was already in the attic. My mom told me that when she was pregnant with me the rose split in two and she put mine in a safe spot in my grandparents' attic. Clearly, my mother didn't know any other details either."

He does have a point, and maybe it could work. Though, my mom ate the flower when it wasn't attached to her yet. Obviously, my rose is connected with mine. I found that out the hard way when my father possessed Hudson and started to rip off the petals. With the flower connected to my heart, I don't think eating my own heart would cure the curse.

I give a curt shake with my head. "I can't. You saw what happened in the attic the other day. If I pull off the final petal of my rose, I will rip my own heart apart."

"There is no other rose left?" he asks and starts to glance around the room.

"No. My father destroyed my mom's rose. I have no idea what happened with the petals after it happened." I release a deep sigh of disappointment.

This is still getting us nowhere. Why is this so hard to solve?

"But your grandfather mentioned he kept everything. Your mother refused to let him get rid of anything related to the rose. After she died he obviously would still honor her request because he loved her. He must have kept it 'cause that is what she would have wanted, right?" Hudson's piercing eyes make me want to believe his words.

I chuckle at the thought. Why would my grandpa keep something like that? "That would be bizarre. I don't think he would."

"We have to make sure," Hudson grunts.

He moves the planchette to "goodbye" and simultaneously says, "Goodbye."

His fingers leave the board and he gets to his feet to glance around.

"What are you doing? We could have asked more questions to get answers from the board," I snap, a bit irritated at the way he stopped without thinking things through.

"Shush," Hudson murmurs and before he places his index finger against his lips he adds, "I hear something."

"Probably my dad, that's nothing new 'cause you said he's been following you around all day," I grumble.

We were so close to getting more answers, I still can't believe he abruptly decided to say goodbye and leave the board. He shoots me a glare, and then his gaze shifts in the direction of the mirror. He jumps back as if he's spooked and almost knocks down one of the candles behind him.

"Watch it," I yell, afraid he'll start a fire if the flame comes near all the scattered papers and boxes stored here.

"I swear I just saw your mom. I didn't see her face, just the pink dress she was wearing earlier today when we saw her in the mirror at the cabin. She didn't say anything but walked right past the mirror or something." His voice is a bit shaky.

"That can't be. I haven't seen her up here since my father made an appearance," I tell him.

"I swear it was her," Hudson states.

A loud bang echoes through the room and the both of us practically jump out of our skin.

"What was that?" I whisper, my heart still racing in my chest with a jolt of adrenaline coursing through my veins.

"Was that there before?" Hudson questions and points at a small box.

I slowly shake my head and take a step closer. I have never seen it before in my entire life. Was that the loud sound we heard? But what made it fall to the floor? And where did it come from?

Before I can say anything Hudson dashes forward and scoops it up.

"Be careful," I warn and stay frozen to my spot.

"You need to take a look at this," Hudson stalks toward me and shoves the box into my hand. "It's sealed with wax."

His finger points at the red wax around the box's lid, sealing whatever it is inside.

"I have no idea what it is or what it could be." I bounce my gaze between Hudson and the box.

This is incredibly weird. Not only to have this box enter the attic out of nowhere with a loud bang, but the box itself as well. What on earth could be inside it?

"I caught a glimpse of your mother's reflection in the mirror before we heard it fall. Maybe she had something to do with it?" Hudson quips.

It's one theory, I have no clue if it's true.

"I'm sure it's a sign or has something to do with all of it. Come on, open it then we'll know," he suggests and wanders off to grab one of the candles.

I huff and drag my feet as I follow him and plunk down onto the floor next to him. Hudson carefully holds the flame of the candle against the red wax and lets it melt away. It takes a while before all of the wax is melted away.

"It still won't open," I murmur.

"Maybe I can pull it open with force." Hudson places the candle back on the floor and takes the box from my hands.

He grips it between his fingers and brings it close to his chest to pry it open. He huffs and uses more force, but it stays shut.

"You're too obsessed with it." I snort. "As if there would be an old rose in there so you can make me eat one of the petals to undo what my mother did decades ago."

I roll my eyes and try to play it off as a joke, because this is getting us nowhere.

The lid breaks and it gives Hudson a chance to see what's inside. His eyes widen when he takes in the contents of the box.

"What is it?" I question and step closer.

It could be anything if it's been up here for years. Grandpa likes to buy lots of odd things and store them in the attic.

"I'm obsessed, eh? You shouldn't have joked about it, honey." There are twinkles of mischief in his eyes when he gives me a sly smile.

I gasp. "No way."

Leaning forward, I glance into the box and my breath catches. That can't be. It's the remainder of my mother's flower. The shredded petals, the stem, all dried up…but it's there, sealed inside for all these years as a treasure.

"Told you," Hudson says with a huge grin on his face.

"I can't believe it," I murmur. "This is…this is my mom's rose."

I place my fingers against my mouth as I stare at it. So it was my mother who Hudson saw a glimpse of in the mirror. She was the one who made the box fall so we would notice it. I glance at the mirror but she's not there. My gaze shifts to the board and I notice the planchette is on the "yes" instead of on the "goodbye" letters where Hudson left it.

"You should eat one of the petals," Hudson says from beside me.

I glance up at him and whisper, "But what if I make it worse?"

Dread fills my stomach. There's no way to know what might happen. My mother became sick when she ate a petal and then the rose was linked to her. The rose is already linked to me through the blood of my mother.

"Why would your mother give you this if it would make it worse?" He raises his eyebrow.

"I don't know, maybe it was my father who is messing with us. You never know who you're talking to when you're playing the Ouija board." The hairs on the back of my neck stand on end when I think about all the things that might go wrong when you're not using a Ouija board correctly. Demons, evil spirits, haunted objects, whatever is out there that can cling to you.

Not only that, but…really? Eating a rose that was clearly cursed. Drenched with whatever poison that was in an old bottle that my father knocked over and spilled onto it. No one knows what was in there. My father didn't say anything because he was a kid and afraid, but what if it's gotten even worse over the years? The petals could be deadly by now.

"If something happens, then we will handle it and figure out what to do next," Hudson firmly tells me. "Together."

I can't help the smile that slides across my face. "We make a pretty good team together," I whisper, and feel my cheeks heat by my admittance.

Hudson leans forward and catches his lips with mine. I close my eyes and get lost in the warmth of his kiss. How does this guy make me feel adored, special, and grounded? Knowing I'm not alone in all of this gives me strength and determination.

He pulls back and croaks, "We're a solid team, honey. We'll get through this no matter what."

The confidence in his movement when he grabs one of the petals and holds it up for me to take.

"If this goes wrong, I'm gonna blame you," I grumble with fake annoyance.

Hudson snickers. "Keep that in mind for when we know for sure this worked out. Then I'll gladly accept your apology and will make you grovel so you know I'm always right."

I roll my eyes, feeling some of the stress fade, and I'm sure he joked around to make me feel better. I take a deep breath and mentally prepare myself for what I'm about to do. There's no guarantee, but I guess I have little options left at this point. Who knows, Hudson might be right and by doing this we can reverse whatever was done to my mother to connect the rose to us.

Warmth surrounds my other hand when Hudson links his fingers with mine. He gives our joined hands a squeeze and I feel confident enough to lift my other hand and bring the petal to my lips. Opening my mouth, I pop the petal inside. A burning sensation hits my tongue when I start to chew.

"Are you okay?" Hudson's worried voice has me squeezing his hand in reassurance for the both of us.

I hope to hell I won't pass out while I chew on the petal that tastes as if it's rotten. There's an awful taste in my mouth and the burning sensation is spreading throughout my mouth as if I'm having an allergic reaction.

"It's gross," I manage to choke out and I try to give him a hint of a smile, but it's so damn hard with the horrifying taste in my mouth as I swallow it all down.

"Yeah, no surprise there." He shoots me a wink.

"So, now what?" I ask.

Nothing happened and I don't feel anything. Okay, it wasn't fun, eating an old petal that's been inside a box for years, but at least I'm not sick or feel weird...yet.

Hudson shrugs and glances around. I follow his gaze but nothing seems out of place. When I turn to look at him, he's just staring mindlessly at something in front of him. An eerie feeling overwhelms me when he keeps staring and doesn't respond when I squeeze our joined hands.

ARTSY

"Hudson?" He doesn't so much as twitch.

Worry settles in my gut and I try again. "Hudson, what are you doing?"

He keeps staring dead ahead and doesn't respond.

"What are you looking at?" I question and start to step around him to see his face.

Why is he acting like this? He hasn't had anything and simply stares straight ahead. Shouldn't I be the one acting weird? Instead, I feel fine and he clearly doesn't. However, Hudson has nothing to do with the curse of my family.

I'm turning to face him and notice how his eyes aren't green like they normally are...they are completely white.

"Holy crap. Hudson!" I scream and grab his shoulders to shake him, hoping to snap him out of whatever this trance-state is.

He looks exactly like he did when he was possessed. This can't be happening. Not now. I knew eating the petal would only cause more problems.

"Artsy." His mouth moves and my name might fall from his lips, but his voice is completely off.

Dark. Twisted. Not Hudson at all. My hands fall away from his shoulders and I take a step back.

"Who are you?" I croak.

"I'm sorry for everything that happened. I was blinded by revenge, by self-hatred. I knew I was the one who spilled the poison onto the rose. I never saw who the rose was sold to and didn't know at the time I met your mother that it was her who owned it. Not until I found the rose in the attic. I panicked. I knew the affect it would have and knowing it was my wife…my daughter." A pained expression falls across Hudson's face and I know my father is possessing him to be able to talk to me.

A whirlwind of emotion assaults my body. Knowing as a kid my father caused an accident that led to this point in our lives. Though, on the other hand, he went berserk and things gravely escalated, and he killed my mother, himself along with it. Then, years later he came after me.

"How did you know that it was the same rose that you poisoned? If you were a little boy when it happened. How did you know it was the same one?" I question, ignoring his excuse and the weak explanation.

"I was at the store a few days after your grandfather returned to the store. He was trying to gather information about the rose and had a picture of it with him because his daughter wouldn't let it out of her sight. I caught a glimpse of the picture and I knew it was the same rose I spilled the contents of the poison on. Your grandfather explained that she ate one of the petals and fell ill. There wasn't anything I could do." His head drops and he gives it a tiny shake when he continues. "Throughout the years I completely forgot about it. When I met your mother I didn't know she was the girl who ate the petal from the flower I poisoned. I didn't see the girl, I only saw someone arguing with my father, showing him a photograph…and I saw that and knew it was about the rose. So, I didn't know…not until years after you were born…until I found the flower. My whole world crumbled within that moment."

His hand reaches for my face and he gently cups my cheek. "I never meant for any of it to happen. It's all my fault. When I saw that rose in the attic, all the horrible memories came back and my mind short-circuited. I had to end it. It's an abomination and you were tainted with it as well. Your mother ingested the poison of the rose and was linked to it. Tainting her blood, passing it on to you. It was a mistake, Artsy. One I've deeply come to regret."

My eyes burn and I can feel tears spill.

"I understand. But I can't forgive you," I croak.

Leaning into his touch for a heartbeat or two, I pull back and keep my gaze locked on him. I wish I could forgive him. He's my father. But how can I forgive a man who killed my mother? Who wanted to kill me? Now that I know the complete background of everything, I understand how it might have caused for him to freak out. Yet, there were so many other options and choices he could have made that wouldn't have resulted in their death. And for that I cannot accept his apology.

He gives me a sad smile. "It's okay, Artsy. I am glad you are the strong woman you've grown into. It's good we all know the entire story now. If I could do it all again there would have been so many things I would have done differently. Sadly, we can't change the past and I'm finally facing the consequences. I've found clarity and only wish I've found it decades ago. Have a good life, Artsy."

His words cause my heart to ache. I didn't think I would cry over the loss of my father. I hated that man for killing my mother. I've never seen him any other way, but now I know his side of the story and that does give a different spin on everything. Even if the result is still the same. At least he sees it too and realize his blind eye to reality, causing him to stop his revenge and urge to kill me as well.

"Goodbye, Dad." I wipe the tears from my cheeks as I give him those words.

A grateful smile appears on his face, as if he made amends.

"Thank you," he whispers in a soft voice and I can see the shift in Hudson's face and his eyes turn from fully white back to his comforting green irises.

"You're welcome," I murmur, knowing very well he's already gone and won't be able to hear it. But I had to say it for myself.

"What happened?" Hudson shakes his head. "Are you okay? Why are you crying?"

He reaches for me and scoops me into his arms to hug me tight. I didn't even know I was crying again, but now I'm sobbing into his chest. I feel as if the weight of the world just fell off my shoulders. After a while I pull back and stare at Hudson's gorgeous green eyes.

"It's over," I proudly tell him.

"He's gone?" Hudson says, excitement clear in his voice.

I bob my head. "Yeah, he left. We talked and he found his peace."

"We did it," Hudson states and whirls me around.

A giggle rips from me and when he stops spinning us, he crashes his mouth against mine. The kiss fills me with warmth, and I relish in the happiness flooding my veins.

Breaking the kiss I repeat his words, "We did it."

I am thankful to have him with me every step of the way. Until now I hadn't even realized how much he has done for me. Through all of this I've doubted his decisions, hated the way he did some things and even wanted to keep my distance from him. All the while he's been doing all of it to help me.

Stunned, I tip my head back and ask, "Why did you help me?"

We went from standing on opposite sides to hanging around, becoming friends, and ultimately lovers. He put himself in a position where he put his own life at risk in an effort to help save mine. All without a second thought.

"You wouldn't believe me." The corner of his mouth twitches and he gently slides a strand of hair behind my ear.

"Try me," I challenge and raise my eyebrow.

"Once we got close, I saw a side of you I wanted to explore. I saw the things that were happening in your life and deep in my gut I felt that it was wrong to have you face all of it by yourself. We connect, Artsy. You've been my inspiration. I've always noticed you, but now? Now I see you, all of you. I didn't want anything to happen to you so I had to help you…for myself as well." I can see the truth in his eyes as he stares into my eyes.

I frown and let his words wash over me. "But…you bullied me."

How could he always notice me? Me, his inspiration? I still can't wrap my mind around it.

Hudson chuckles. "To get your attention, sweet Artsy. It's hard not to notice you when I park near the tree you're always sitting against. The first time I said something to you the guys laughed and it just spiraled from teasing to nagging you to notice me too I guess. It's hard to balance all the things in life. Being the popular guy, the band, my friends, the girl I'm attracted to. Can't have all so I try my best to pull all the strings. Though, when I saw them hurting you? The shit got out of hand and I put a stop to it. Finally I had the guts to grasp my feelings and make it real between us. I'm glad I did, because now you're mine."

My heart skips a beat while my chest fills with the warmth his words give me. "I always hated myself for having a crush on the guy who bullied me. But I guess I wasn't alone with my feelings."

"You should have stayed at the concert so you heard the end of my song." He squeezes my hip and pulls me even closer to his body.

"Why? How does the song end?" I breathe and get lost in the intense look in his eyes.

"Let's save that for later, alright?" He slides his thumb over my bottom lip, spreading tingles all over my skin.

"But, I can say with confidence that we were meant to happen." He leans in to close the distance between us.

"I guess we were," I whisper and close my eyes when his lips brush against mine in a whisper of a kiss.

He pulls back with a frown on his face.

"What's wrong?" I wonder.

"Maybe you should brush your teeth first. You know, after eating that gross decade's old petal." He looks serious for a fragment of a second before he laughs.

I smack his chest and murmur, "Idiot." Then I wince, knowing I have a bad taste in my mouth so I also think he's right. "Yeah, I totally need to do that."

He snorts. "It's fine. I was just teasing you." He leans in to place his mouth next to my ear. "But if you deny me a kiss and will brush your teeth first, then it'll just give me an excuse to ravish your mouth later."

Heat floods my body and I want nothing more than to rush into the bathroom and brush my teeth so I can let Hudson kiss me. My gaze wanders over to my rose, or where it's supposed to be.

"My rose," I gasp. "Where is my rose?"

"What?" Hudson whirls around to follow my line of sight. "Do you think it vanished after you ate the petal?"

He gives me a confused look, but his guess is as good as mine.

"Maybe." I keep staring at the empty spot.

Why would it completely vanish? How? It just doesn't make sense. Did my father take it with him? Did we break the curse by making him see the error of his way? Setting his spirit free or something like that?

"I think…we made it come full circle. The end. Poof, that's it, folks," I joke.

Hudson chuckles. "I think we did."

I take a deep breath. "I can't wait to tell my mother about this."

Even if she warned me about the rose and not to ask any questions, and only keep it safe…I still think she'd be proud to know that we solved it. The rose is gone and I'm still alive, without a threat out in the open. No one can destroy my rose and me along with it.

"Should I give you some privacy?" Hudson asks and takes a step in the direction of the door.

"Thanks, I'd appreciate it. Can you wait in my room? I'll be down in a bit," I tell him and I give him a smile.

I'm glad he understands me and the connection I have with my mother. He shoots me a wink and backs out of the room. After everything that happened in the attic it feels weird to stand here now without fear. It feels safe and normal again.

I turn to face the mirror and squat down to sit in front of it. Something I've done each and every day for years.

"Hey, Mom," I start and look at my own reflection as I wait for her to appear behind me.

Usually, when I call out for her it doesn't take more than a minute or two before I hear her voice or see her. But this time it stays silent and there's only my reflections staring back at me.

"Mom?" I swallow hard, afraid something happened to her.

Why isn't she responding? She always comes when I call for her.

I try again. "I need to tell you something, Mom."

She can't be gone. Everything is supposed to be back to the way it was except for the rose. No more evil spirits, no more rose linked to my heart. If giving up the curse means I have to give up the link with my mom? Then I don't want it solved anymore. We need to go back to how it was. I need her. I need my mother. This can't be happening.

My chest tightens and I feel my eyes overflow with tears of sadness.

"Mom," I cry out her name. "Please." My voice breaks and a sob rips from my throat.

I stare at my own reflection and hate the void I'm left with.

"Come back," I shout and jump to my feet to rummage through the boxes.

On the bottom I notice a rock I painted when I was a kid and I grab it. Turning to the mirror I realize there's nothing left. My parents are gone, just like the rose, and the curse. No link left that ties them to me. I guess I won't be needing the mirror either if she isn't going to show up again.

My grief, thoughts, and emotions are taking over my decisions. Pulling my arm back I get ready to shatter the mirror with the stone I hold in my hand. Before I can hurl it against the mirror there are loud footsteps and a strong body colliding with mine.

"What are you doing?" Hudson grunts and I collapse in his arms.

Sobs rip from me and I barely manage to croak out the words, "She's gone."

Saying the actual words causes a sharp pain inside my chest. I can't believe I didn't think about the consequences of getting rid of the curse. The flower was the only link I had with my mother; the only way that made me see my mom.

"Artsy," Hudson whispers, and gently rubs my back.

I look up at him through my blurry vision. "I don't want this."

"I know, but she was with you to protect you. She watched over your rose, your heart. We made sure the curse is gone and now your mother doesn't have to protect you anymore. She's finally able to find peace," he explains with a gentle voice.

His words make sense, no matter how painful it is to know he's right.

"Do you think she's in a good place now?" I wonder.

He rubs his thumbs over my cheeks to wipe my tears away. "I like to think she is. But who knows, she might find a way to visit you again. Give her time while you give yourself time to grieve and heal."

Hearing him say these words to me feels as if he grabbed a string and needle and sewed all my wounds together.

Right now I don't think I can live without ever seeing her again. My mom has been there for me no matter what. It's painful to know I won't be able to talk to her. I told my father goodbye, I didn't have a chance to do that with my mom. I just wish I could see and talk to her one last time.

"You will see her again. One day, I'm sure of it," he repeats.

I nod and dry my eyes. I wish I believe him, and all I can do is hope. Though, with Hudson by my side it will give me the strength to pull through and fight for what I want in life. Just like we did the past few days. We will figure it out. Together.

A HEART DOOMED BY FATE

EPILOGUE

ARTSY   *Ten years later*

I put my hair into a bun on top of my head and give myself a final once-over. My makeup is done, clothes perfect, and I just finished my hair. Stalking to the closet, I stand on my tiptoes and reach for the leather vest to take it with me. Finally, I grab my purse and rush down the stairs and glance in the direction of the living room.

"I'm ready to go," I yell at Hudson.

"Great, me too," he replies as he saunters toward me.

In his hands are the last couple of bags, and yet he still manages to open the door for me. After breaking the curse, I had a hard time and avoided going outside or talking to other people. My grandparents were worried about me, even more because they didn't know what happened.

Hudson suggested moving in with me, due to the fact that he was the only one who managed to make me talk. He made it his personal mission to make the smile grow on my face, even if it was a tiny one at first. For him it was good enough.

My grandparents saw the change Hudson brought upon me and were happy for us. Everything went better after he moved in. He forced me to go outside with him, to take a walk, or to go out shopping, to the fair, and I also got to visit his parents for the first time.

You could say Hudson saved my life more than once. Though, after all these years living with my grandparents, it was time for us to move into our own place. We searched a long time for a house that we both liked and could see us living in for many years to come. It took a while but ultimately we found our dream house.

"Looking beautiful," he murmurs in my ear as we step outside and he closes the door behind us. "Like always."

"Oh, shut up," I reply on a husky chuckle and take one of the bags from his hand to walk to the car.

"Ten years together, and I still can make you blush," Hudson states with a hint of pride in his voice.

I roll my eyes, but inside my body fills with warmth. I still love him fiercely after all these years together. There's never a dull moment between us. He's my rock, and I'm his inspiration, or so he says. We complete one another and share each other's strength to stand tall and face whatever hits the path life surprises us with.

Hudson shoves the other bags in the trunk while I watch him and slowly put on the leather vest. He turns to face me and I can tell by the way his eyes widen that he recognizes it.

"Is that?" he croaks.

"It sure is." I grin and turn slightly to show him the back where the rose is embroidered into the leather.

"I can't believe you still have it." His eyes fill with warmth and I know he's thinking back to the night he gave it to me.

When he sang the song he wrote about me. The night we kissed, had a confrontation, and he followed me home. It's the night our adventure really began. There is no way I would get rid of this leather vest. The memories alone made me keep it.

"It fits you perfectly." He smirks and lets his eyes wander over my body in appreciation.

"Better than you," I reply with a hint of challenge in my voice.

He shakes his head and laughs it off as he closes the trunk. Hudson gets behind the wheel while I also take a seat.

"Ready?" he questions and starts the car after putting his seatbelt on.

I give him a brilliant smile and tell him, "I can't wait."

Hudson guides the car onto the road and I open the window to let some fresh air in. I watch the content smile on his face as he drives toward our new home. We've spent a lot of time fixing it up, moving stuff in, and today it's finally time to call it home.

The ride to the new house is nice and reminds me of the time when he used to take me for a drive to get me out of the house. With his help I managed to pull through grief, emotions, and depression. I'm not afraid to glance back and think about how far I've come. How far Hudson and I have come. We're a team. Partners, standing shoulder to shoulder to carry our worries and problems together and fight through them to find a solution.

He parks the car in front of our house and turns his head my way. "I have a little surprise for you."

"What is it?" I ask, unable to hide my excitement.

"It wouldn't be a surprise if I told you." He snorts and gets out of the car.

Opening the door, I step out and close it when I ask, "Okay. So, where's the surprise?"

"Inside," he states and walks around the car to open the trunk to get the bags.

I let my mind wonder over all the possibilities, but to be honest? I have absolutely no idea what his surprise could be. I open the door of our new home and let Hudson inside so he can put down the heavy bags. Coming home makes me smile.

The house is big, yet cozy. It's filled with stuff we bought together and it's really our place that feels like home.

"Ready for the surprise?" he questions, and I can hear the happiness in his voice, the same that runs through my veins as well.

"Yes," I squeal, overexcited about everything this day brings.

"Close your eyes," he tells me and walks away to fetch the surprise.

I do what he says and close my eyes as I stand in the middle of the living room with a huge smile on my face. I can hear by the sound of his footsteps that he's coming back to me.

"Okay, put your hands out," he orders.

Slowly, I bring my arms up and place my hands palms up. There's no one on this planet I trust more than Hudson. I feel the weight of a bundle of fluff being placed in my hands. My heart skips a beat, secretly knowing exactly what I must be holding.

"No way." I gasp and let my eyes fly open.

I'm holding a gray kitten with white stripes. She's tiny with her bright eyes that have the color of the sky, and her fur is so incredibly soft. Ever since Hudson moved in with me at my grandparents' house, he kept telling me that he would give me a cat as soon as we got a house together. He knows I've always wanted one, but with everything going on with my life it was never the right time to take care of one.

"What's her name?" I let my gaze find Hudson and quickly glance back at the cat who I'm now cuddling against my chest.

"Tara," he states with a gentle voice.

I swallow hard at the sound of the name. "Tara," I echo, and know it definitely suits the bundle of fluff.

"We can change it if you want," he says with a hint of worry in his voice.

"No," I quickly tell him. "I like it. It suits her."

"She has the exact same eyes as your mother. She reminds me of her," Hudson states. "That's why I thought the name of your mom would suit her perfectly. She's the one who eventually brought us back together. I thought it'll be a nice way to honor her."

He is right. I swallow down the emotions clogging my throat.

"Do we need to go out and buy her stuff?" I question to change the subject.

The corner of his mouth twitches. "I already bought everything. No worries."

I place Tara onto the floor and she bows her back and stretches before she rushes off and dashes up the stairs.

"She's fast," I remark and run after her to make sure she won't tumble down the stairs or gets herself into any problems upstairs. I hear Hudson laughing and muttering something about me worrying too much.

I reach the top of the stairs and notice that she's nowhere to be found.

"Tara?" I call out and wonder where she's rushed off to.

A soft meow flows through the air and it's coming from our bedroom. I smile and walk down the hall, but when I enter the bedroom, she isn't there. She meows again, but this time it's more clear. There she is, sitting in front of the mirror looking at her own reflection.

I giggle and squat down behind her to pet the soft bundle of fluff. "It's a beautiful mirror, isn't it? It was already here when we bought the house. Hudson only cleaned it and painted the frame."

My eyes are locked on my own reflection when I catch a hint of a long pink dress behind me. I gasp and shoot a glance over my shoulder but there's nothing there. Trying to calm myself, I take a deep breath. It must have been my imagination. When I turn back to face the mirror the glimpse of a pink dress is back.

"Hello?" I whisper while my heart is racing inside my chest.

"Hey there, Artsy," a familiar voice says on a whisper.

It's sweet and loving, and my heart instantly calms by the sound of her voice.

"Mom?" I croak and feel tears well in my eyes as I bring my fingertips up to my mouth, stunned by the reflection I see behind myself.

She's really here, just like all those years ago in the attic of my grandparents or whenever I needed her, she would appear as a reflection.

I haven't seen her in ten years, though.

"How? Why now? Just...how?" I stutter, not understanding how or why this is happening.

"Do you know where you are, sweetie?" my mom asks.

I'm still blinking my tears of joy away. I must be dreaming. I gave up on ever seeing her like this. I sought out every mirror, looked at every reflection, and still there wasn't a trace of her for over ten years. Why now? Our first day in our new house and she shows up. There's no magical connection, no rose, and no reason for her to be here. It's a newly built house.

"Home," I state and feel the kitten crawl onto my lap. "This house was just finished, Hudson and I moved in today."

"That is right, it's a new house. But that doesn't mean this place doesn't have a history." A smile flashes across her face.

I've missed her smile.

"I don't understand," I murmur. "What history could a new house have?"

"The ground of this street used to be buildings with different stores. They tore down the buildings and built houses instead. The house you and Hudson picked to live in is in the exact same spot the flower shop from your grandparents on your father's side was located. It's a beautiful spot, don't you think?" she explains to me.

I can feel my eyes widen. Wait. Did she just mention the fact that our house is sitting in the exact same spot of the flower shop? The one where it all began? The rose, the poison, it all happened on these grounds. Except, there's no store or connection left, only a new house that was built in the same spot.

"How is it possible that you are talking to me? There isn't anything left from the shop. I tried to communicate with you in the attic like I always used to do. I even went to the little abandoned cabin in the forest a few times over the years. You never showed," I rattle, trying to understand why she's here now after a decade of staying away.

"Why did you keep a dirty mirror you found in the garden of a new house?" she fires back with a grin on her face. "This mirror used to hang in the shop. Why do you think you were drawn to it when you saw it? Everything happens for a reason, sweetie."

I never thought the mirror was connected to anything from my past, let alone from the flower store. When I saw it in the back of the garden hidden in the bushes and covered in dirt, I thought it was a waste to throw it away. I asked Hudson if he could fix it, and he agreed to do it for me.

"Does this mean you're going to stay with me?" I have to ask, I can't lose her again.

The smile fades from her face. "I want to, but I saw how far you've come, and how strong you are on your own. You deserve to have a life with Hudson without any worries or anything holding you back. You've grown so much, and I am incredibly proud of you for how you've dealt with the situation you were in. It meant so much to me when I saw you talk to your father and faced everything head-on. I'm glad you know the complete story, even though I told you to leave it alone. I am glad you chose not to listen to me and you're on your own way in life."

She places her hand on my shoulder. I see it in the mirror, but I can't feel her connection or warmth. Though, it feels good and it still warms my heart to know she's with me right here and now.

"I need you," I croak, and it reminds me of the exact same thing I screamed in the attic when I noticed she wasn't with me anymore.

"No, sweetie, you don't. I will forever be with you in your heart and thoughts. Hudson will take care of you. He's a good choice, Artsy. Really, he already fought hard for you and he's willing to give up everything for you." My mother gives me a proud smile.

"Thanks, Mom." I smile while a tear slides down my cheek. "There's one question I have to ask."

"Sure." She nods and waits for me to pop the question.

"Did you find peace?" I try to take in her expression, but it's hard to do when she's a faded reflection.

"I did. Knowing you are happy is what brings me peace. Have a good life, Artsy." My mother blows me a kiss.

"I love you, Mom," I murmur and feel the tears now fall freely.

It's hard to let her go. Yet, this time I did get to say the words I wished I could've told her ten years ago. Her reflection completely fades away and I'm back to staring at myself. I'm wearing a huge grin, happy how we left things between us. My mom is happy, and I got the goodbye I wished for.

"That was perfect," Hudson states from behind me, dragging me back to the here and now.

I turn around and notice the unshed tears in his eyes. I bet he listened to the entire conversation.

"I got to say goodbye," I tell him, still not believing I got the opportunity to do so.

"You did," he states proudly and walks toward me. "I'm glad you found the mirror in the backyard and asked me to clean it up. Guess it was worth all the work," he jokes and scoops Tara from my lap and holds out his hands to pull me to my feet.

"It definitely was." I grin and lean in to brush my lips against his.

I still can't believe how a decade ago we were standing on opposite sides. The girl with a crush on her bully while struggling to keep going with the havoc in my life. One moment caused a change. A connection that grew stronger, and I don't think I'd be here right now if it wasn't for Hudson.

We've come so far, and to see him standing before me with the little kitten in hand, I know we have our whole lives still ahead of us. Ready to start a family. Released from the curse, and free of our worries. Because whatever difficulties we'll face, we'll handle it together.

With my past settled, and closure when it comes to both my parents, it leaves the future wide open for the life I always wished for, but never thought I deserved. It still blows my mind to be this lucky to have Hudson beside me as my friend, my partner, my lover, and future husband.

Such an unexpected turn in my life to end up with my bully. Was it worth the struggle to overcome everything? Yes, yes it was. Everyone needs a second chance, and it was worth forgiving him when he ran after me, soaked to the bone by the rain. I forgive him for everything, because in time he became my everything.

A HEART DOOMED BY FATE

MAZE

Thank you for reading A Heart Doomed By Fate!

Gaining exposure as an independent author relies mostly
on word-of-mouth, so if you have the time and inclination,
please consider leaving a short review wherever you can.
Even a short message on social media
would be greatly appreciated.

For more MAZE books, go to:
https://books2read.com/rl/Maze

Printed in Great Britain
by Amazon